HARD TO FORGET

Blazing Eagle Ranch 5

PEYTON BANKS

There are still a few men who love
desperately.

— J.D. SALINGER

BLURB

Trouble follows her wherever she goes. He's a man willing to prove his love for her.

Nykee Nash returned home to Shady Springs a changed woman. No longer was she the juvenile delinquent who committed crimes and broke the law. Nykee had paid her debt to society and wanted to move on with her life. She threw herself into her new passion and was the happiest she had ever been.

Until Karl sauntered through the door of her newly established business.

Around Karl, Nykee began to live again.

Karl Tanis didn't know what hit him. One look in Nykee's warm brown eyes, and he was a goner. Karl had heard of her past but believed everyone deserves a second chance. He had spent most of his life working a ranch and was no stranger to hard work.

He was up for the challenge to wrangle in Nykee's heart.

She's stubborn, but he's confident he will win her over. But with a twist of fate, everything they had came crashing down around them.

Nykee doesn't want him anywhere near her now, refusing to let him help fight her battles. There's no way he is leaving her alone. He will not give up on their love because she would be hard to forget...

$$\text{❧}\quad\text{I}\quad\text{❦}$$

"Hey! Sheldon, no biting." Nykee Nash was firm with her words. She stared down the giant husky standing on her grooming table.

He threw back his head and howled as if to try to convince her he didn't need his hair cut.

"Your momma will be here soon, and we have to have you cut and looking good," she said. She bit back a laugh when he rolled his eyes. Huskies were extremely intelligent, and Nykee was a firm believer they understood human language.

"I thought that was Sheldon's voice." Korah chuckled, walking by. She carried a white Bichon toward the shower stalls.

"Yeah. His mom said they were getting family

photos and she wants him to look his best." Nykee turned back to Sheldon and eyed him. He whined again before finally standing still in defeat.

"That's cute," Korah said. She secured the dog she was working with and bustled around gathering what she needed.

"It is." Nykee reached for her shears and began trimming his coat to even it out. His almond-shaped blue eyes were locked on her. They held a mischievous expression, alerting her that he was going to bless them with his infamous howls and dog language.

Her lips curved up in the corner while she started snipping faster. She loved every moment of her job. She glanced around and took in the grooming shop.

This was all hers.

What the Fluff.

She had always loved animals, and when she had returned home, she had decided to open a pet spa and grooming shop. She was really good at what she did, and she was so blessed that she was able to fulfill a dream.

Sheldon kicked his leg out away from her. She had better hurry. His mother, Sharon, had started bringing him a little over a year ago. Sheldon was used to their grooming ritual, but he was still impatient.

"Few more minutes." Nykee bit her lip and picked up his paws to clean up his pads. After she'd finished the last one, she stepped back from him with her hands up. "We are done, you handsome boy."

His tail whipped back and forth, and he even smiled.

"Wait, one more thing." She snagged some Burberry cologne that was pup-friendly and gave a few sprays to make sure he smelled wonderful. "Now we're done."

"Looking good there, Sheldon," Korah said.

Sheldon barked.

"I was just coming back here to see if he was done," Blake said from the door. He was one of the groomers she employed. He was helping out at the front desk today since their receptionist, Nora, was out sick for a few days.

"He is. Give me a couple of seconds," Nykee replied.

"Okay." He disappeared just as quick as he'd peeked his head in through the door.

She slid a brand-new collar on Sheldon, and then he was ready to go home.

"Let's go, boy," she murmured. She assisted him down to the floor. He was a beautiful husky who was a very friendly dog, but now he was anxious to see his mom. She walked him out to the front of the shop with him whining and pulling the entire way. He took one look at his momma and went crazy.

"Oh, there's my handsome boy." Sharon bent down and rubbed Sheldon behind his ears. He barked while licking her face. "Oh, someone smells good."

"That's the Burberry cologne," Nykee shared.

"I love this one. It's one of my favorites." Sharon stood to her full height and took the leash from Nykee. She turned back to Sheldon who was demanding attention. "You're such a handsome boy. Nykee has you looking amazing."

"You have to show me the pictures." Nykee offered her a small smile. She was glad her client was happy with her work, but then again, Sheldon was a handsome dog.

"We will."

Nykee took care of her payment and secured Sheldon's next grooming appointment. Once Sheldon and Sharon were gone, she faced Blake who had finished a telephone call. "You hanging in there out here?"

"Yeah, I'm good. I just hope Nora is okay." He swiveled in the chair toward her.

"I spoke with her this morning. She should be back to work in a day or two." Nora was one of the first people she had hired when she had opened What the Fluff. Nora had come highly recommended by Nykee's father, Louvell.

"That's good." The phone rang again, and Blake snagged it.

Nykee took a peek at the schedule for today and saw there was an appointment later for one of her favorite clients, Daisy the Frenchie. Her owner, Billie Tanis, was a wonderful woman who spoiled the pup.

She gave a wave and headed toward her office. She went inside to work on a few things. It was a Monday, and it was not as busy. She closed her door and sighed.

This was her safe space.

Nykee sat at her computer and toggled the mouse to wake it up. She always felt a sense of accomplishment when in her office.

She had been through a lot.

Nykee wasn't ashamed of her past, but she tried to keep it there. It wasn't too long ago that she had been a troubled woman. As a teen, she had hung out with the wrong crowd, and her life spiraled out of control.

Nykee had fallen under the spell of Foster Moss. A savvy-talking criminal who had set his sights on her. She was young and had believed everything he said. He had made promises that a naïve girl trusted. He could do no wrong.

He'd taken advantage of her.

Anything he'd asked, she'd done.

But her family never gave up on her.

Even when she ran away.

Got in trouble with the law.

Paid her debt to society with a five-year stint in a women's prison.

Her family never stopped loving her.

It was when she was enrolled in a rehabilitation program in the prison where she could learn to take care of dogs and even groom them that things had changed. The program was not only for the inmates but the animals as well. They would be soon adopted after completing the program.

The first dog she had encountered was an abandoned stray pit bull named Libby.

That's when something in Nykee had clicked. It was as if she had found her calling. She had always had a love for animals, and her heart was captured by those big brown eyes. She'd felt good knowing she could help an animal look their best and help them get adopted.

Nykee had thrown herself into the program and thrived off it. She now had a sense of purpose in life.

She had spoken with her parents about opening up her own grooming salon, and they'd backed her.

She had left prison a reformed woman and with a plan.

Within a year, What the Fluff was opened. Two years later, she had a nice clientele list that allowed her to grow and hire two great groomers and a secretary.

Nykee blew out a deep breath and glanced around her office.

She was now a businesswoman, no longer a criminal. She had left that person she used to be back in prison. She wasn't the naïve young girl but a strong woman who was cautious around those she didn't know. It had taken a while for her to warm up to her employees.

She liked them all and appreciated them, but it hard for her to trust that they were people she could count on.

Thanks to Foster; he was the reason she had trust issues.

But she was still a work in progress.

"We're not thinking of the past now," she murmured. She shook her head and focused on the information on the screen. She had too much to do to give Foster any more of her energy.

Throwing herself into her work, she ran through

her local marketing. Getting the word out about her business had been hard at first. Residents of Shady Springs hesitated about hiring her. She faced opposition to her business because of her past.

The one thing about living in a small town, everyone knew everything about you.

She had worked hard to show that she was a changed woman. The clients she did have were wonderful, and she appreciated them all.

Now she had to work on gaining more so she could grow What The Fluff.

The phone on her desk rang. She snatched it up and answered. She knew without looking who it would be.

"Nykee, baby. How are you?"

Her father's, Louvell Nash, boisterous voice came onto the line. He called her every day around the same time just to check in on her. He and her mother were her rocks. Her father was an accountant and helped her with her books, which she appreciated. He had taught her so much about running her company.

"Hey, Daddy. I'm doing well. How's your day going?" she asked. Nykee looked forward to these calls. She had grown extremely close to her father. She was the youngest of three children, and he always made her feel as if she were the only one. Not that her older brother and sister didn't feel the love. Their father was just one hell of a man, and to put up with everything she had put him through, he was definitely going to Heaven.

The man had the patience of a saint.

"Good. I had lunch with your brother today, and we were talking about you."

"Really? I hope all good."

Her brother, Jimar, was the oldest of the three and the most responsible. He had graduated from high school, went to college on a football scholarship, graduated, opened his business, and married his high school sweetheart and had two little kids. His life was perfect and something she hoped one day she could have.

"Always good. We were laughing, remembering the time you had got caught letting those greased pigs loose in the high school." He snorted.

She cringed, recalling that day. She had been in the ninth grade and started hanging with new friends. One of the kid's parents owned a pig farm, and they were able to steal some of them and release them into the school. Just trying to grease up ornery pigs had been a task in itself.

She had got suspended for a few days. Her father had thought it was hilarious.

That was one of her pranks that had begun her

downward spiral. First it was crazy pranks, and soon it moved up to theft and vandalism.

"What brought that up?" She offered a dry chuckle.

"We were leaving the Farmhouse Diner and saw a kid walking down the street with a pig on a leash."

"What?" That drew a giggle from her. That would have been a sight to see.

Her father went on to talk about his and her brother's lunch conversation. Her brother was wanting to have everyone over for dinner. Their sister, Bashara, who lived in Chicago with her husband and children, would be coming home to visit.

Nykee perked up at that. She hadn't seen her sister in a few months, or the kids. She loved being an auntie. She got to spoil her nieces and nephews then send them back with their parents.

She was the cool aunt who the kids loved hanging around with.

"Let me know when Bashara is coming, and I'll make sure I'm there."

"Well, what else do you have to do, my dear?" His innocent question was like a kick to the gut. She was the only one of his children who wasn't married and giving him and her mother grandchildren.

She sat up straight. Seriously? She hated when he

and her mother got on their high horses about her not being settled down yet. "Well, you do know the life of a—"

"You know I'm just joking with you." His tone dropped, and she felt like a heel for getting defensive. He sighed, and she could hear every one of his sixty-two years in his voice. "I just want you to be happy. I'm so proud of the woman you have become. All of those trials and tribulations you went through was God's plan."

Her shoulders slumped. Of course her father would want the best for her. How could she think otherwise?

"I know, Daddy. I'm happy being the cool auntie at the moment." She laughed.

"You're like a magnet. Everyone is drawn to you. Especially those kids. You've got a big heart, and people sense that. Even those animals you love to work with. You know they say animals have a way to sense good in people, right?"

She definitely knew. Animals were what had helped her get her life together. They didn't judge, and they loved unconditionally.

She clicked on the tab at the top of her screen that she always kept up. It was the website to the local animal shelter. She had been thinking of adopting a dog. There were some cuties that had caught her eye.

If she did get one, then she'd have someone to talk to when she was at home, cuddle with during bad storms.

Right now, that sounded good. It would be nice to have someone devoted to her and offer her love.

❧ 2 ❧

"**O**kay, Miss Daisy. We are going to go for your appointment, then I'm to take you back home." Karl Tanis glanced over at the French bulldog who stared at him. Her oversized round ears stood up on end, and her big brown eyes watched him with an intelligence that showcased her personality. The little dog had spunk and was the perfect companion for his mother.

Here he was, thirty-five years old, a big, tough ranch hand for one of the largest spreads in the state, taking his mother's dog for her grooming appointment.

"And why don't you travel in the back seat?" he asked. She let out a bark and rolled her eyes. She turned away from him and tried to stand her front paws on the door so she could look out the window. "Yeah, you're just like my mother."

He shook his head and coasted his truck to a stop. They were almost at the destination. He'd seen the grooming shop before but had never gone in there. His mother treated this dog like one of her children, and according to her, Daisy needed her bath and nails done.

He sighed.

He didn't know how he'd got roped into doing this.

His mother only had to bat her big blue eyes, and he and his brother would do anything for her.

"Daisy is your little sister," Billie had said. She was unable to bring the dog for her appointment because she was needing to go with her mother to her doctor appointment and she had some errands for the family cookout they were throwing.

Karl should have volunteered to take Gram to the appointment.

But according to his mother, since he lived in Shady Springs, he could do this. His parents still lived in his childhood home a few towns over in Beckton. His mother had heard of the groomer here in Shady Springs and only used them for her precious dog.

He guided his truck into an empty parking spot

in front of the store. Daisy barked and began getting excited.

"You must like this place," he muttered. He eyed the crazy dog while he killed the engine. He focused his attention on the building and chuckled.

What the Fluff.

Whoever had come up with the name of the business was certainly creative.

She barked again and turned to him, waiting.

He grabbed her leash and picked her up. He reached for his Stetson sitting on the back seat and plopped it down on his head.

"Let's go." He exited the vehicle and slammed the door shut. He didn't see anyone he knew on the street. They were in the midst of downtown Shady Springs. There were plenty of shops, other businesses, and a couple of places to grab coffee or food.

He sat Daisy down on the ground, and she took off walking. He refused to carry her along. God gave her four good legs to use. His mother carried her around a lot, claiming the dog's legs would grow tired if she walked too far.

She appeared to be walking just fine.

They arrived at What the Fluff and went inside. The reception area was warm and cozy. It reminded him of a salon. There was a guy with short blond hair sitting behind the counter.

"Welcome. Can I help you?" The guy gave him a nod.

"Yes, I have Daisy Tanis here for her appointment." Karl's voice grew gruff. He stopped in front of the desk and leaned his hip against it. He glanced around and found a woman sitting reading a magazine. He didn't see a pet with her, so he assumed she was waiting.

"Daisy Tanis," the receptionist murmured. He typed out a few commands on the keyboard. "Okay, yes. I have her appointment. She's here for a shampoo, conditioner, facial scrub, and a pawdicure. Is that correct?"

Karl stared at him as if he were speaking another language.

What was a pawdicure? And the damn dog was getting a facial?

Only his mother.

Too bad Billie never had any girls of her own. They would have been spoiled rotten. Not that he or his brother, Kaden, had a bad upbringing. His father, Briggs, and Billie both doted on their boys. They'd had a wonderful childhood, and their family was close.

"I have no idea. She's my mother's dog, and I'm just to drop her off."

"Yeah, Mrs. Tanis always gives Daisy the works

when she comes in." The man laughed. He stood and leaned over to look at Daisy. He greeted her, and the dog barked back as if to respond. "We have Mrs. Tanis's credit card on file. Is that what we're to use?"

"Sure." Karl shrugged.

"Okay. Let me notify her groomer. It will be one moment." The receptionist picked up the phone and placed it to his ear. He dialed a number then paused.

Karl's cellphone buzzed in his pocket. He pulled it out and found a message from his mother.

Invite Nykee to the cookout.

He frowned. Who the hell was Nykee? He replied with the question.

Daisy's groomer. She's a doll, and I'd love to have her come.

Karl sighed and replied he would. He wasn't surprised that his mother had extended an invite. She was a social butterfly and loved making friends. He slid his phone back into the breast pocket of his shirt.

"Nykee will be right out. You can have a seat if you like. She said give her a minute or two."

"Thanks." He moved over to a chair and took a seat. He stretched out his legs. He'd been working a ton of overtime on the ranch, and his body was tired. He adjusted his hat back away from his eyes. Daisy came to lie on the floor by his feet.

The door to the business opened, and a young kid walked in with his German Shepherd. He walked over to the desk to check in. Karl eyed the big dog. Now that was a manly dog. He peered at Daisy who was staring at him with a sassy expression in her eyes.

"Don't give me that look." He grunted. She rolled her large eyes and rested her head on her front legs. He leaned his head back on the wall and shut his eyes. He was tired and felt drained. Today was his day off, and he had planned to meet the guys for a drink and maybe go home and crash.

Unless he found a pretty little gal who wouldn't mind some after-hours fun.

He ran a hand along his jawline and grimaced at the stubble that met him. He would need to clean himself up a bit. He had no problem finding someone to warm his bed. It had been a while since he'd had a steady relationship. One-night stands had been convenient for him with as much as he worked.

He wasn't opposed to relationships. He just hadn't found the right someone.

"Well, hello there, Miss Daisy," a soft husky voice said.

Karl opened his eyes, and his heart lurched. He couldn't help but stare at her. She was a knockout. She had the most beautiful warm brown skin, large brown eyes, and her hair drawn back away from her face with a headband. She was dressed in jeans with a smock covering her shirt. He caught sight of a few tattoos on her inner forearms and had the urge to want to see them up close and personal.

Her gaze connected to him, and what little air he had in his lungs was ripped out. Daisy tugged on the leash, trying to get to the woman. She knelt in front of the dog and ran her hands along her back.

"You must be Billie's son," she said. Daisy barked and jumped around, apparently excited to see the woman. The woman stood and offered her hand to him. "I'm Nykee."

"I'm Karl. Um, yeah, Billie's my mother." He stood and removed his hat. His mother would box him in the ears if he didn't stand for a lady. He rested it against his chest with one hand while he took hers in his other one. Daisy's leash dropped to the floor.

The second they touched, his heart fluttered.

What the hell was that?

He stared into her eyes and was able to see she guarded herself. She had a smile for the dog but kept herself reserved around him.

"She asked for me to bring her dog in for her appointment." He cleared his throat and took his hand back. He found himself tongue-tied around her like a young lad talking to his first girl.

A small smile graced her lips as she bent down and picked up Daisy's leash.

"Well, since this is your first time bringing Miss Daisy for her puppy spa appointment, you can come with me." She waved for him to follow her. Daisy trotted along with her. She paused at the door and turned to look at him.

"Oh, I have to come back there?" His feet finally began to move. They had been rooted in one spot. He'd caught sight of her ample bottom highlighted by her jeans. Thick hips and a nice ass were his weakness. He grabbed the handle and opened the door for her.

"Yeah. There are a couple things you need to pick out. It's part of the package." Her eyes crinkled in the corners, and she appeared as if she were trying not to laugh at him.

Frankly, he wanted to see her smile. He wanted to see her relaxed and happy. He wasn't sure where this thought came from, but he could tell she didn't smile often.

"Would I be the best person? Can you call my mother? I wouldn't want to pick out the wrong—"

"It's simple. I promise." She led him down a hallway to a little alcove with a computer.

"Okay." His gaze dropped back to her ass, and he swallowed hard. He'd follow this woman anywhere.

She stopped in front of the computer and motioned for him to stand next to her.

"We need to choose a color for Miss Daisy's nails." She clicked a few keys and brought up a color palette on the screen.

"What?"

"Her nails. She's getting a pawdicure." Nykee leveled him with her gaze as if this was an important decision to make. She wiggled her fingers in his direction, showing off her fire-engine-red painted nails.

His gaze dropped down to them. He inhaled sharply, willing to admit he had a thing for women and their nails. There was something about a woman trailing her nails down his naked back... He drew up short and bit back a curse.

"Every girl needs a color for her nails."

"Oh, um." He leaned in closer to the screen to get a better look at the colors. He inhaled, catching a whiff of Nykee's light floral perfume. He wanted to nuzzle his face in the crook of her neck and breathe it in.

He jerked back.

What the hell was he doing?

He tightened his hold on his hat and shook his head. He had to get a grip, or this woman would think he was either a creep or crazy.

"How about this one." He pointed to a blue color. He glanced over at Nykee for her approval.

She gave a nod and clicked on the color. "Good color. Curious Blue will be great on Miss Daisy." She leaned down and gave the dog a rub on her head. "Want me to pick out her perfume?"

Relief filled him.

"Please. My mom trusts you, so whatever you choose, I'm sure she will be happy with it."

Nykee straightened and returned back to the computer. She clicked a few more things before she closed out the program she was working on.

"Miss Daisy will be done in about two hours. Will you be picking her up?" She bent down and lifted Daisy up.

Daisy grew excited, yapping and trying to plant a big kiss on Nykee's face.

"Yeah. I will." He ran a hand through his hair before putting his hat back on. He had been so caught up in trying not to drool over her that what his mother had asked him to do just about slipped his mind. "I almost forgot. My mother wanted to invite you to our cookout we are having."

"Really?" She patted Daisy's head. The dog had settled down and leaned into her.

"Yeah. We do this once a year where we have a huge shindig at a nearby park. She invites practically the entire county and wanted to make sure you were invited."

"That's sweet of Billie." She hesitated, her gaze flicking to the dog. She dropped a kiss on top of Daisy's head.

"If you don't say yes, she'll probably blame me for not asking you right." He chuckled. There was no way he was leaving without her agreeing to come.

"No she won't." She gave him a side-eye in disbelief.

"Oh, she will, and I can't leave without you saying you'll come." He wasn't above a little guilt trip. It wasn't just his mother, but he wanted her to come. He wanted to get to know her.

Everything about Nykee intrigued him.

"Billie is such a good client, and she always refers her friends to me." She chewed on her lip while thinking.

He bit back a groan at the sight of her tugging on her bottom lip.

Yeah, he needed to go out and have several drinks with the guys. He had never had this strong of a reaction to a woman before. She wasn't even flirting with him, and it left him second-guessing himself. He was used to smiling at a woman and having her fall all over him.

Nykee barely acknowledged him.

Was he losing his touch?

"So, you'll come." He grinned, turning on the Tanis charm. He and Kaden were used to using their good looks to get what they wanted.

"Yes, I'll come. Where will the party be?" She blinked a few times at him and frowned.

Shit, he *must* be losing his touch.

She pulled out her cell phone and inputted the address into it along with the details.

"Are you okay?" he asked. He couldn't help it. There seemed to be something wrong with her. This was the first time they'd met, but there was something about her. He didn't want to leave without making her smile.

"Um, yeah. I'm good, why?" She tilted her head to the side and watched him wearily.

"I don't know." He shrugged. He slid his hands into his jean pockets. He met her gaze and refused to glance away. He craved to see her smile.

No, he wanted to be the *reason* she smiled.

"You just seem...sad. I hope you have a beautiful day and that there will be something that will make a pretty girl like you laugh."

"And just that quick after meeting me, you can sense things about me?"

"I'm pretty good at reading people...horses... It's sort of my job or I could get hurt." He didn't even want to think of the near misses when it came to ornery cattle, bulls, or horses. He had to be able to read a situation and body language.

Looking at Nykee, it was easy to see she didn't trust many people.

For some damn reason, he wanted to be one she could count on.

ykee stared at the cowboy and didn't know how to respond. It wasn't often that someone asked about her. But for some strange reason, he was able to pick up on something that she kept to herself.

No, she didn't trust many people, and he knew it.

She wasn't sure how she felt being compared to horses and such, but she guessed he had a point. Working with certain animals could be dangerous. She knew he worked at the Blazing Eagle Ranch from his mother bragging about him and his brother.

He had a charm to him, and he was definitely aware of it and used it.

He was handsome.

Okay, more than that.

He was downright droolworthy, but she knew

what that meant. He would be a heartbreaker. She'd had enough of men who used their good looks to get what they wanted.

She'd promised herself when she'd sat in her tiny jail cell all those years that she'd never let herself get taken advantage of again.

Nykee bent down and picked up Miss Daisy who was standing on her hind legs trying to get her attention. Holding the dog gave her something to do with her hands. She was comforted by the feel of the dog in her arms. Karl's presence was slightly overwhelming. He was a big man, but he wasn't using his size to get his way.

"I'm not sure what you want me to say, but I'm fine." She shrugged. She slid her hands down Daisy's back. "I guess I would just need something to laugh about."

"Hmm...is that so." Those hazel eyes of his piqued with interest.

Oh boy.

Did she just issue a silent challenge without thinking?

Her heart pounded at the closeness of him. She didn't know what his cologne was, but it smelled nice. Her body was definitely responding to the nearness of a handsome man.

He was tall and fit. His plaid shirt did nothing to

hide that he was muscular. Not gym muscles but those created from hard physical labor.

"What is that supposed to mean?"

"I'm just thinking. A woman like you needs to laugh. What time do you get off?"

Nykee took a step back. She eyed him and acknowledged to herself that she was attracted to him.

It had been years since she'd been with a man.

She didn't even want to think of Foster.

What that was—it hadn't been a healthy relationship. She didn't even know if she knew what that would feel like.

"Are you, um, asking me on a date?" she breathed.

Miss Daisy let out a yip, jerking her attention to the dog. She must have tightened her hold on the poor pup.

Karl slid a hand through his dark hair and leveled his gaze on her.

Her breath caught in her throat.

She was in trouble.

"I'm meeting some friends for drinks and figured you could tag along."

She chewed on her lip, trying to think of an excuse.

Did she have anything to do after work?

Nope.

The only thing she had planned was searching online for the pet shelters to see if she could find a pup to rescue.

Her hands grew sweaty. Karl didn't know her background or that he was standing in front of a woman with a dark past. When she'd moved back to Shady Springs, it hadn't always been easy.

She'd received looks, heard whispers, and she tried to ignore it.

People who she had thought where her friends didn't want to have anything to do with her when she'd returned from prison.

Her parents had encouraged her to get out and meet new people. Hell, even her therapist challenged her to do something like this.

What would it feel like to just go out after work, have a drink, and share a few laughs?

"Are you sure your friends wouldn't mind if I came? I wouldn't want to intrude."

He barked a laugh and tipped the brim of his hat back. The move was simple but downright sexy.

"They won't mind. The more the merrier." He patiently waited for her to make her decision.

You need to get out of the house.

She blew out a deep breath and wasn't sure if this was going to be a mistake.

"I'll come. It sounds fun."

His grin spread across his face. Her heart stuttered at the magnitude of his smile.

Karl Tanis was a heartbreaker all right.

She was going to have to protect herself around him. This was just an outing to make new friends.

Nothing else.

She wasn't sure who she was trying to convince.

Herself or her vagina.

❧

"YOU LOOK MARVELOUS, MISS DAISY." NYKEE stood back to admire her handiwork. The Frenchie was one of her best clients. She always appeared to enjoy her time at the puppy salon. "You get a treat for behaving so well."

Daisy's ears twitched at the word treat.

"Don't she just look like a little star." Korah chuckled. She turned back to cleaning the showers down.

It was the end of the day, and Daisy was the last client. Nykee pulled a treat out of her smock and offered it to Daisy who promptly took it. Nykee was always amazed how well animals behaved when they knew treats were the reward.

"I know." Nykee placed the pup down to the floor and guided her over to the waiting cage.

"I didn't see Ms. Billie today. Who dropped Daisy off?"

Nykee's face grew warm at the thought of Billie's son, Karl. She closed the latch and turned around, walking back to the table.

"Um, no, she didn't drop off Daisy. Her son did."

"Oh, which one? Billie shared photos with me of her boys, and they are sexy." Korah giggled.

"Um, Karl."

"Ooohhh! The cowboy." Korah sighed. She dried her hands on a towel and strolled over to Nykee. A dreamy look appeared in her eyes. "What I wouldn't give to ride that cowboy."

"Korah." Nykee rolled her eyes. She wiped down the table and pushed off the hair onto the floor. She would need to finish cleaning up before she left. Her hands shook slightly thinking of meeting Karl and his friends.

"I'm sorry, boss lady. I can't help it. You did see him, right?" she asked.

"Of course I did. I spoke with him, too." She tried to block her reaction to him from her mind. She would try to remain professional in front of Korah. Even though Korah had no filter when she spoke. Nykee didn't mind her outspoken employee. Sometimes she wished she could be like Korah. She was young and had her whole life ahead of her. She was a good girl and never got in trouble.

"Then you know what I'm talking about." Korah grinned. Her shoulders slumped when she realized Nykee wasn't going to join in discussing how handsome Karl was. "Oh, come on, boss. Lighten up, I'm just having fun."

"I'm just tired, Korah." Nykee already knew her employees didn't consider her fun. Which she would admit hurt a little. She had so much weight on her shoulders that she couldn't afford to mess anything up. Being an ex-con didn't leave much room for anything. She was always judged by her past. No matter how hard she worked, someone always had to bring up that she had served time in prison.

"Do you have any plans for tonight?" Korah grabbed the broom and began sweeping.

"Actually, I was invited to meet some people for drinks after work," Nykee admitted hesitantly. She walked over to check on the trash and found them already emptied. Her employees were the best. They were hardworking, and she was lucky to have them.

"Really? Good for you."

"Thanks." Nykee glanced around and found the work area was spotless. She hadn't realized Korah had been tidying up. She slid her hands down her pants and gave a nod.

"Hey, Nykee. Daisy's ride is here." Blaze peeked his head through the door.

Nykee's heart skipped a beat.

Karl was apparently a man who was prompt.

"I think I forgot to vacuum the waiting area." Korah flew out of the room and disappeared through the door behind Blake.

Nykee shook her head and took Daisy out of her crate.

"What is wrong with that girl?" she muttered.

Daisy gave a bark and tugged her to follow Korah. Apparently, everyone was excited to see Karl. She ventured out of the workshop area and strolled toward the front. Her hands grew sweaty in anticipation of seeing him again. She tried to regulate her breathing and slow it down.

She didn't know why she was so nervous around him. Karl appeared to be a down-to-earth guy, but there was something about those hazel eyes of his that had her panties in knots.

Maybe she shouldn't go.

She wasn't ready.

Yes, she'd cancel and stay home to search online for a puppy to adopt. That would be much safer.

Her mind now made up, she stood tall when she walked out the door that led to the waiting area.

Karl's intense gaze landed on her, and all thoughts escaped her.

What had she just been thinking about?

"There she is. Nykee has Daisy looking her best. Billie is going to be so happy," Korah exclaimed. It didn't escape Nykee's notice that Korah was trying to catch Karl's eye.

Karl pushed off the counter and stood to his full height.

Damn the man for being tall and handsome. His lips spread into his sexy grin, but his attention wasn't on the dog, it was on her.

Nykee arrived in front of him and handed him Daisy's leash.

"Perfect timing. She's all yours," Nykee said. She cleared her throat, unsure why her voice was low and husky.

"I hope she behaved herself." Karl's eyes crinkled in the corners. He pushed his hat back away from his eyes and leveled her with his gaze again.

"Yes, she's a real diva and enjoys her spa days." Nykee rubbed her hands on her pants again and inhaled.

"It's not often that most pups don't." Blake chuckled. He stood from behind the counter and stretched. "I can't wait for Nora to return. Desk duty is hard."

"Oh, please. I'll cover it tomorrow. It's not that bad." Korah giggled.

"We're still on for today, right?" Karl asked.

Korah's and Blake's heads whipped around to them. Nykee refused to look at either of them. She already knew she would see the shocked expressions on their faces.

"Well, see about that." She slid her hands into her pocket.

"Aww...come on. It will be fun. I've already told the guys, and my boss will be bringing his wife. You won't be the only woman. Promise."

His eyes were pleading, and Nykee recognized the sensation rolling through her chest.

She always was a sucker for a good-looking man, and Karl was downright gorgeous.

Go. Have fun. He's not asking for anything but time, a little voice in the back of her head whispered.

"Sure. I'll just need to shower and change my clothes. I probably smell like dog." Nykee looked down at herself.

"Great." He backed away, tugging Daisy with him. He glanced over at Blake and Korah who were standing with their mouths gaping open. "The bill is settled, right?"

"Um, yeah. We'll charge Billie's credit card," Blake answered.

"Great." He opened the door, and Daisy stepped through it. He tossed Nykee a wink. "See ya later."

He disappeared through the door with it closing slightly behind him. She watched him walk past the wide glass window until he was no longer visible.

"That's who you have plans with?" Korah screeched. She jumped up and down before bolting over to Nykee. She wrapped her up in a hug, laughing. "What are you waiting for? Get out of here, boss. We'll lock up."

"Are you sure—"

"Yes!" Blake and Korah hollered simultaneously. They both had shit-eating grins on their faces.

"It's not what you think. He's inviting me out with his friends for drinks and—"

"It doesn't matter." Korah's smile disappeared. She rested her hands on Nykee's shoulders. "You need this. I know you've been through some stuff and don't really socialize much, but if you didn't know, we all care about you here and want to see you happy."

Nykee's throat closed up on her. She coughed a bit, feeling the burn in the back of her eyes. She was really lucky with her crew. They were the best, and she felt bad for not opening up to them much.

"Thanks. That means a lot to me," she said.

"Korah's right. Go have fun. Have a beer or two

for me." Blake came around the corner and slapped her on the back.

Nykee relaxed and smiled. "Okay. Beer has never been my thing."

"Then one of those fruity girl drinks y'all like to sip on." He laughed.

"We expect a full report first thing at work tomorrow." Korah smiled and stepped back from Nykee. She pointed to the door. "Now go. Get out of here!"

❧   4   ☙

"If you look at the door one more time, I'm going to assume we're not interesting anymore," Parker's voice cut through Karl's thoughts.

He whipped his head back around and grinned. Karl reached for his ice-cold glass with his frothy brew in it and shrugged.

"The boss gets to grace us with his presence tonight, we'll take it." Karl chuckled. He raised his glass and tipped it to Parker.

It wasn't that often Parker was able to come out and hang with them. He and his wife, Maddy, now had their second baby. With running the ranch and an additional child, it left little time for Parker to hang out at bars.

"I was finally able to convince him to let Wade

and Joy watch the kids." Maddy laughed. She leaned into her husband and rested a hand on his chest.

The grumpy rancher's face softened when his eyes met his wife's.

Karl wouldn't mind that type of reaction from a woman. Parker was a hard-nosed ex-bull rider, but when it came to his wife and kids, he was a softy. That son of theirs, Tyler, had Parker wrapped around his little finger, and their daughter, Emma Grace, was the same.

Karl was envious of Parker. Everyone on the ranch knew the story between the two of them. Ten years they were separated with Parker not knowing he'd fathered Maddy's child. Karl couldn't even imagine finding out information like that. He was sure it would have ripped him in two. Apparently, Parker had thought Maddy had just left him, while in reality, Parker's old man, Jonah, had a hand in separating the two because he hadn't thought Maddy was good enough for Parker.

Karl shook his head and took a hefty sip of his beer.

Where was she? They had been at the Tipsy Cow for at least a half hour now, and no sign of Nykee. She'd probably bailed and decided not to come. He'd seen her hesitate earlier when he'd asked her again if she was coming.

"Who are we waiting on again?" Darnell asked. He leaned back and popped a boneless wing in his mouth.

"Nykee. Nykee Nash. We met earlier. She's my mom's dog groomer, and I invited her out to hang."

"Wait. Nykee Nash?" Maddy frowned. She glanced over at Parker before leaning away from him. She sat forward and tucked a stand of hair behind her ear. "I know you aren't from around here and I'm not one to gossip, but she has a history."

"What are you talking about?" Karl paused. Shady Springs was a small town, and everyone knew everyone, but he had never met Nykee before today. What was Maddy hinting at?

"Look, anyone from Shady Springs knows of her from when we were in high school. There were some stories floating around—" She paused and shook her head. "You know what, never mind. I'm sure she's not the same person she was back then. Just forget I said anything."

Karl's curiosity was piqued. Everyone had something in their past they weren't proud of. He wasn't one to judge someone from past mistakes but by how they were presently.

There had been shadows in Nykee's eyes.

Calm down.

This was a friendly invite to get to know her, have a few drinks and laughs.

Not a date or anything.

The way she had acted when he'd first asked her had him thinking she would have turned him down flat if he had been trying to take her out. Out with the gang seemed like it would appeal more to her.

There was something about her that drew him to her. Their first meeting had been short, but it had certainly left a lasting impression on him.

"Karl can take care of himself." Parker wrapped an arm around her and brought her back against him. "From what I heard, she's doing well for herself, Maddy girl."

"I just want him to—"

"Maddy," Parker's voice dropped low.

She stopped and looked at him. Karl smiled at the wife of his boss. She was always protective of them all. She was like the momma bear of the ranch.

Karl's attention was snagged by movement at the door.

"I'll be right back." He pushed back from his chair and stood. He threaded his way through the crowd toward Nykee. His heart rate increased at the sight of her.

She scanned the area, and when her gaze locked

on him, he felt an electric current shoot through him.

She was absolutely breathtaking.

Her dark hair was left down, and light makeup adorned her face. In Karl's opinion she didn't need it, but the red shade of lipstick on her lips had him wanting to taste them. She was dressed in a black top with jeans and a pair of knee-high, black heeled boots. She played with the strap of her purse that crossed her chest while they stared at each other.

"You made it," he breathed. He tried to not act too overzealous. He really hadn't thought she was going to come.

"Yeah, I said I would." She nervously reached up and pushed her hair behind one ear. She had the look of a deer caught in headlights.

"Everyone's waiting to meet you. Want to grab a drink first?"

She jerked her head in a nod. He moved closer to her and rested a hand at the small of her back and guided her over to the bar.

"Whatever you're drinking on is on me," he offered. He elbowed a few guys out of the way to give them room at the counter. He raised his hand and caught the eye of the barkeep.

"Really?" She leaned against the bar and faced

him with one of her eyebrows raised. "And this isn't a date?"

"Nope. Just a friend buying a drink for another friend." He tossed her a wink. He was going to have to be careful with her. She was suspicious of him. He didn't know who had hurt her in the past, but he sensed she was well worth the wait.

"Who said we're friends?"

"Ouch." He ran a hand along his jawline. The girl sure knew how to bust his balls. She stared at him with her wide brown eyes. He gave a shrug. "Well, my mother did invite you to our family cookout, and that would mean by default we would be friends."

"Is that so?" She bit her lip, and a small smile ghosted her lips.

"Yeah." He grinned and leaned closer to her. His confidence was growing. That tiny tilt of her lips was all he needed. "I'm sure I'll grow on you."

He was breaking through her cold shell. He was going to get her to relax and downright smile if he had to try all night. The barkeep made his way down to them. She placed her order and glanced over in the direction of the table where everyone was waiting for them.

"Those are your friends over there?"

"Yeah. They are dying to meet you."

"I'm sure they are." She turned to take her glass from the bartender.

He took out a few bills and slid them over to the guy.

"Come on, so you can meet the gang." He took her by her hand and entwined their fingers together. He knew he was being forward, but he couldn't help himself. There was something about her that drew him to her.

He was a natural flirt, but he was going to have to work harder with her. She wasn't like any of the other women he'd been involved with.

Two times they'd been in the presence of each other, and he was already wanting more.

And he did take notice that she didn't remove her hand.

Laughter filtered through the air from the table. Maddy giggled from something Darnell said. They paused and turned their attention to Karl and Nykee once they arrived at the table. Nykee slipped her hand from his as she stood next to him.

"Nykee, this is Parker, his wife Maddy, and Darnell." He pointed to each of them.

"Hello." Nykee offered them a small smile and nodded to them.

They all returned a smile and greeted her.

"This seat is for you." Karl pulled her chair out for her.

She sat and flicked her gaze to him. Karl sat next to her in his abandoned chair.

"Thanks."

"So you own What the Fluff?" Darnell asked. He leaned forward, resting his elbows on the table.

"I do," Nykee replied.

"I always did think that was a clever name." Maddy laughed. "How did you come up with it?"

Karl settled back in his chair and breathed a sigh of relief. He wasn't sure what Maddy had been hinting at earlier, but he was glad whatever it was, she put it aside.

Nykee relaxed and played with her glass that sat on the table in front of her.

"Well, it's a crazy story. I was trying to come up with a catchy name and was drawing a blank. My brother and his family came to visit. My nephew, who was about four at the time, wanted to go out in the backyard to play. I didn't mind so I took him outside. Out of the corner of my eye, a large bird came swooping down and snatched a squirrel from the yard. In my panic and trying not to curse, I grabbed my nephew and the words what the fluff came out of my mouth."

Chuckles went around the table.

"Yeah, I don't know if I would have been able to stop cursing thinking an eagle was trying to come after my nephew," Darnell said.

"It was instinct. Adam had been mimicking and saying what we say. There was no way I could have Jimar know I cursed."

Karl couldn't take his eyes off her. She was the most beautiful woman in the building.

So what that she had a past. Karl was only interested in her present and future.

❧

NYKEE HAD A THING ABOUT PEOPLE-WATCHING. IT didn't take long to see that Karl and his coworkers were close, if not friends. Their stories were crazy and some downright unbelievable, but she guessed that life on a ranch could be that extreme.

Time had gotten away from her. She glanced down at her watch and saw a couple of hours had passed. She was enjoying herself and was on her second, maybe third drink. She didn't know when she'd asked for others, but the waiter must have kept dropping drinks off.

The food at the Tipsy Cow was good. She made a mental note to come back here and grab dinner or lunch to go.

"So I don't know if you remember, but we went to high school together," Maddy said. She offered Nykee a smile.

She did look familiar to Nykee, but honestly, she couldn't place her. High school hadn't been the best of times for her. She'd run with the wrong crowd and had barely paid any attention to anything in school. She was more focused on having fun with her 'friends' and being in trouble.

"Oh, we did?" Nykee gave a nervous chuckle. If Maddy remembered her from high school then that meant she knew her background. Nykee tried not to grow defensive. Ever since returning to Shady Springs, she'd had to defend herself and try to prove that she wasn't the same girl she'd been when she'd left.

"Yeah, I think you were two years behind me." Maddy rested her glass down on the table.

"Those were crazy times. I can't say I remember much from those days." That was the safest thing Nykee could say without revealing to Karl that she had been a wild one back in the day. She glanced over at him and found him curiously staring at her. Seeing him in this relaxed environment did things to her.

Hell, even at her shop, she'd been turned on by his smile and the twinkle in his eyes. It didn't help that he was physically fit and smelled good.

Nykee honestly didn't want him to know what kind of person she had been. But she knew that wasn't reality. He was going to find out that she was an ex-con with a criminal past.

She just hoped he wasn't like everyone else.

Lose interest and ignore her.

That would hurt.

She wasn't sure why she cared what he thought of her. Since prison, she would like to think she had thick skin. She had paid her dues to society and was now an honest citizen.

"High school days are behind us all. Can't say mine were the best." Karl snorted.

"What?" Maddy gasped.

"We all weren't like Parker. Football and bull riding." Karl tilted his glass toward Parker.

The quiet rancher tipped his Stetson back on his head and leveled his intense glare on Karl. He was a big guy, and Nykee could easily imagine him wrangling a bull with his bare hands.

"Fuck you," Parker muttered. He shook his head and picked up his mug, waving it in the air. "But look at you now. You work on the best damn ranch in the state of Colorado."

"Hear! Hear!" Darnell and Karl echoed.

"When I was in high school, I was about shy of

six feet and skinny. I might have weighed a hundred fifty pounds." Karl snickered. He leaned back and rested an arm on the back of Nykee's chair. "I was teased unmercifully for it, too."

"Really?" Nykee blurted out. It was hard to believe. She couldn't help but skim over him and found everything perfect. He had certainly bulked up and grown taller. She was five foot five and had to tilt her head back to meet his eyes. "How tall are you now?"

"Last physical I had, doc told me I was six-three." A sexy grin spread across his lips.

Nykee's heart skipped a beat at the twinkle in his hazel eyes. He patted his stomach, and her gaze dropped to his abdomen. It left her imagining what he looked like without a shirt on. "Eating all my vegetables certainly paid off."

Nykee had to bring her thoughts back from the gutter. Imagining him with no shirt on was certainly heating her up. Her core clenched at the fantasy of running her tongue along the ridges to count them.

"Nykee, you certainly look the same from high school." Maddy laughed. "I'm quite jealous. I gained weight after having Tyler and never could get it off. After baby Emma, I think I put on even more."

"Ain't nothing wrong with your body," Parker

growled. He wrapped and arm around her neck and drew her to him. He dropped a kiss on her forehead.

Nykee bit back a sigh watching the two of them. Anyone sitting within a mile of them could see how much in love they were. Parker appeared to be a hardened rancher, but there was certainly a soft spot for his wife.

"Well, I'm glad you think so." Nykee shrugged. She glanced down at herself. She, too, had gained weight, and the addition of tattoos were new also. She had started collecting them when she'd turned eighteen. Her parents wouldn't sign for them, so she had to wait until she was of age to not need their permission. Foster had tried to con her into getting a few at a couple of 'tattoo house parties,' but she wasn't stupid. If she was going to get ink, it would be professional. "But I, too, gained weight. These hips were not here in high school."

Some chicks in prison took to lifting weights to give them something to do. Not Nykee. She had never been one to indulge in physical activities. Her brother and sister had been into sports. Jimar had been into basketball and track while Bashara was into volleyball and tennis. Nykee was the only Nash child to not play sports or join high school clubs.

"Well, you look good to me." Karl's fingers played with the strands of her hair.

A shiver rippled through her body. She peeked over at him and arched an eyebrow.

"Then you need glasses," she muttered. She knew she had to work on losing weight somehow. Her mother had forced her to establish herself with a local physician, and one of the first things Dr. Young had shared with her was that she needed to lose weight. One hundred and eighty-five pounds was not healthy for her. Not that Nykee had any medical problems.

"Oh, geesh Look at the time," Maddy announced. She turned to Parker and gave him a nudge. "We have to go. I promised Joy we wouldn't be out long."

"All right. It's not like they can't handle the babies. Tyler's there with them," he grumbled.

"Boy, let's go." She gave him another little nudge.

"Yeah, I got to go, too. I have to be at work early. You know that boss of mine is hard-nosed and strict," Darnell joked. He stood and stretched.

In the last hour or so, the crowd had thickened. There were tons of people enjoying their night at the bar. When she'd arrived, she had been surprised there was a bouncer at the door, but it hadn't taken long for her to get in. Security seemed to be tight, and she imagined in a place like this, there must have been a few fights that would warrant them.

She'd grown in up this town and knew from first-hand experience that some people couldn't hold their liquor and fighting always went along with it.

Foster had started his share—

Nope. She wasn't going to continue to think about him. She had moved on and hadn't heard from him in years. No point in allowing him to rent space in her head for free. Once she had gone to prison, he had cut all ties with her.

"Sure am. Better see your ass there at five a.m." Parker grinned. He held out his hand for Maddy to assist her from her chair.

She stood, and his arm immediately dropped around her waist. It was sweet how protective of his wife he was.

Nykee only wished she had someone like that in her life.

"Y'all go ahead. I got the bill," Karl said. He pulled his wallet out of his jeans and flagged down the waiter.

"I can pay for myself," Nykee said. She reached for her purse that hung on the back of her chair. She searched for her wallet, but Karl's large hand settled on top of hers. Her gaze flickered to his.

"Your money is no good here," Karl said. His warm eyes crinkled in the corners. "We take turns picking up the bill for the group. It's what we do, and today's my turn."

He handed the waitress his credit card. "I'd like to settle our bill."

"Sure thing, Karl. Be right back with the receipt," the woman said. She spun on her heels and walked away.

"It was nice meeting you, Nykee," Darnell said.

"You, too," she replied.

Parker and Maddy also said their goodbyes before heading out, leaving Nykee and Karl alone at the table.

Nykee bit her lip and faced Karl. Even though they were in the middle of the bar, it sure felt as if they were truly alone. He had given her attention and ignored the stares from other women who had passed him. He'd laughed at some of her comments and even tried to draw her into their conversations.

He was different, and she could admit, she did like him.

A lot.

"Are you going to be okay driving home?" he asked, nodding to her empty glass.

"Yeah, I'm good." She had sipped on her drinks the entire time they had been there. She didn't have a buzzed feeling at all. If she did, she knew not to get behind the wheel and drive.

The waitress returned with a receipt. Karl quickly

took care of the bill and tip before focusing on her again.

"Come on. I'll walk you out to your car." He stood and then reached out his hand.

She froze and stared at it for a moment then took it.

This was the second time he'd taken her hand in his. She had to admit it actually felt right.

This is not a date, she whispered to herself.

He led them through the bar and out the door.

"Have a good night, Karl," the oversized bouncer said.

"You, too, Derek." Karl tightened his hand on hers.

There were people lined up waiting to get inside the bar. A few women cast their approving stares to Karl, but he ignored them.

"Where are you parked?" he asked.

"Over there." She pointed at her little sedan.

They strolled hand in hand toward her car. She pulled out her keys and hit the unlock button so he'd know which one was hers. They arrived at the driver's side. She turned to him and glanced down at their hands. She rested against the door and tilted her head back to meet his gaze. "So, this wasn't date?"

That sexy grin of his appeared. He stepped in

front of her, trapping her against her car. She didn't feel anything but lust streaking through her body.

Yes, it had been a long time since she'd felt wanted by anyone. Karl had quickly broken through the barriers she had tried to construct to protect herself.

Her body was definitely reacting to his. She bit her lip to stop herself from blurting out the request for him to come back to her place. They were both grown, and two consenting adults indulging in pleasure wasn't wrong.

She didn't want to appear too forward.

"Well, see, this is the thing," he began. He pushed her hair from her face. He trailed his fingers along her cheek, and she found herself automatically leaning into his touch. "When I take a woman out, there would be no question about the intent of the outing."

"Is that so?" she breathed.

"Oh, yeah. See, there is this thing that a man does where he arrives at her house, picks her up, and treats her like a lady." His voice deepened.

She was entranced by his words and held on to every one of them.

Those fingers of his reached her lips and traced the bottom one. "How does that sound?"

She blinked, having to register his words. Her

skin was on fire everywhere he touched. Everything around them faded off into the distance.

"That sounds nice," she whispered.

"How about it? Me picking you up and taking you out. Just me and you."

"Yes," she replied without even thinking. It was a no-brainer. Karl Tanis had her wrapped around his little finger. She didn't care if he took her out to muck stalls, she'd show up. "I'd really like that."

"And I'd really like to kiss you," he murmured. That finger of his rested on her lip with his heated gaze locked on her mouth.

Nykee's hand shot out and grabbed his shirt. She closed the gap between them and stood up on her tiptoes. His head swooped down and captured her lips.

Stars exploded from the feeling of his mouth on hers. Nykee gasped, and he quickly took advantage, slipping his tongue inside her mouth.

This kiss was like no other she'd experienced before. Karl wrapped an arm around her waist while the other one gently cupped her jaw. She slid her hands up him until they dove into his thick hair.

A car horn blared past them. They broke apart but didn't take their eyes off each other. Nykee's breaths were coming fast.

She was in trouble. Her nice little life she'd tried to build for herself that was supposed to leave no room for the opposite sex, crumbled before her eyes.

"Well, if you are going to take me out, then you will need my number."

Karl couldn't get his mind off Nykee. That kiss in the parking lot of the Tipsy Cow had rattled him down to his soul. He had promised her a date and he was going to damn well make sure it was one where they could have fun. He wanted it to be different and something she'd definitely remember.

She'd given him her number, and it had taken everything he had not to call her that night. He didn't want to appear to be desperate, but holy hell, that kiss.

If she would have invited him back to her place or his, he would have taken her up on it.

But there was something in her eyes that didn't sit right with him. He wanted to get to the bottom of it. Everything about the woman was a mystery. He was sure he could ask around, but that wasn't the type of man he was.

When she was ready to tell him what was haunting her, then he was sure she would.

It had been a decent two days, and his cell phone was burning a hole in his jeans.

"Come on, Champ. Time to go," he called out. He gave his horse the command to head back to the stables. They were out on the range, checking on the herd they had moved a few days ago. Champ, his loyal steed, turned around and trotted along. Karl took in the amazing sight of the Blazing Eagle Ranch and fell in love with it all over again. It was one of the largest ranches in the state, and he was a lucky son of a bitch to be able to work it. The Brooks family was hardworking and well-known. He considered himself fortunate that he was able to pull this job.

He remembered the day he had interviewed for the position. There were tons of men who were applying for it. Everyone knew the Blazing Eagle paid good money and took care of their employees. He'd had a private interview with Jonah Brooks, the patriarch of the family. The old rancher had been blunt and straight to the point. He was looking for a man who would carry his weight, was loyal, and had a love of the land.

All which was Karl.

From the time he was a little boy, he'd known he wanted to be employed on a ranch. He loved the outdoors and working with his hands. He was no stranger to backbreaking labor. His father, Briggs Tanis, had instilled that trait into him and his brother, Kaden.

It wasn't long after he'd met with Jonah that he'd found out he'd gotten the job. He'd moved over to Shady Springs and hadn't looked back.

A nice breeze blew, and he inhaled the scent of the outdoors.

His thoughts soon moved back to a shy, brown-skinned woman with big brown eyes. He frowned, thinking of her comment that he needed glasses when he'd mentioned he liked what he saw.

Someone had hurt her.

That had to be the cause of the shadows in her eyes and the mistrust he'd picked up on.

Well, he was going to have to work on that.

It had been a long time since he had wanted to enter a relationship with anyone, and something about Nykee had him wanting to jump headfirst into one with her.

It was close to lunch, and he decided he'd call her while he had time. He and Champ made their way back over to the barn. He let Champ into one of the small corrals to graze and get a drink of water while he ran into the employee barn. He'd grab his lunch he'd packed and call her.

His heart quickened at the thought of hearing her voice. It was Sunday, and he didn't think her shop was open today.

He entered the break room that had been set up for the employees. The Brooks family provided a barn where hands could sleep over if they chose to. It was outfitted with rooms, a little kitchenette, with a few tables where they took their breaks and a full bathroom with shower stalls. There were plenty of times he'd just slept over when he was scheduled back to back. Most hands did during the busy season.

"How's it going, Karl?" Stan was seated at one of the tables, eating.

"Good. What's been going on with you?" Karl asked. He opened the fridge and took his lunch pail out.

His friend grinned and settled back in his seat.

"Life's good." Stan's grin spread over his entire face.

Karl snorted. His friend was another one who had found love. But Karl wasn't jealous at all. Stan deserved it. He'd gone through one hell of a divorce from his wife and now he was remarried to Nasia. His friend was almost a different man after meeting her. He'd fallen fast and hard for her, and Karl was happy for his friend.

"How's Nasia doing?" he asked.

"She's good. Busy as ever with her shop." Stan took a swig from his water bottle.

"We missed you on Friday." Karl grinned and leaned back against the counter. Lately, his friend had been ditching them with the excuse of needing to go home to the wife. Stan was in love and was pussy whipped by his wife. "You could have brought Nasia. Parker and Maddy joined me and Darnell."

"I heard you invited a female along." Stan raised his eyebrows.

He knew Karl's reputation with the ladies. Karl wasn't surprised that gossip had made its way around. More than likely it was Darnell, but he didn't mind at all.

"Someone's been yapping," he muttered.

"You know it was Darnell. He was telling everyone how you couldn't take your eyes off her." Stan chuckled. "Who was it? Anyone I know?"

"Nykee Nash. She's my mom's groomer, and I invited her out just to meet some people." He shrugged, trying to play it cool, but from the expression on Stan's face, he wasn't buying it.

"Sure. So when are you taking her out?" he asked.

"I'm on my way to call her now." He barked a laugh. Yes, his friend knew him all too well. He backed away and spun on his heels. He didn't care that his coworkers were talking about him. Most of them had no room to talk. Everyone had watched Stan fall for Nasia, Rashad for Yani, and the Brooks brothers for all their women.

Why shouldn't he have a turn?

He headed out of the barn and strolled over to a wide tree that overlooked the land. It was one of his favorite spots to come out and eat. He settled down on the ground and opened his cooler. He'd packed a couple of cold-cut sandwiches, chips, fruit, and a drink.

He took a bite of his first sandwich and pulled his phone out. He slid his finger along the screen and hit the contacts button. When he came to Nykee's name, he paused.

What did he say?

He had never been one to second-guess himself around women, but Nykee was different. He wanted to make a good impression on her.

That kiss they'd shared had left him going home to take an ice-cold shower. His dick hadn't gone down until then. He would try his damnedest to go slow with her.

Even if it killed him.

When he finally got her underneath him, or on top of him, he didn't want any shadows in her eyes.

He hit her name and put the phone up to his ear and waited.

"Hello?" Her husky voice came onto the line.

He closed his eyes and bit back a groan. Even her voice did something to him. His jeans suddenly felt too small.

"Nykee, its Karl," he announced. He put his sandwich down and readjusted himself. He was going to need another cold shower soon. Blue balls wasn't going to be a good look on him.

"Hey," she said softly. "How are you?"

"Better now I hear your voice," he murmured.

"Really? And why is that?" she asked.

His heart sped up. Without even seeing her, he could hear she was flirting with him. His lips curved up into wide grin.

Two could play that game.

He was making progress. He'd treat her like a scared little filly, and before she knew it, she would be eating out the palm of his hand.

"Well, for the last few days, this woman with big brown eyes, soft lips, and tattoos on her arms has been on my mind. I can't stop thinking about her," he admitted. He reached over and popped a few chips in his mouth.

"So you can't stop thinking about her? Huh? Then why did it take you so long for you to call?" she asked innocently.

He choked on his chips and had to wash them down with his water. He barked out a laugh.

"Well, ma'am, I'm truly sorry."

"Or were you not talking about me, and already called the woman who you've been thinking about?" she teased.

"I was definitely talking about you." He cleared his throat and took another swig of his water. The smile that spread across his face was sure to be larger than the whole state.

Oh, yeah. Nykee Nash was flirting with him.

"I just needed to make sure you were." A soft giggle escaped her.

The sound of her laugh had his heart all but leaping into his throat.

Karl swallowed hard and shifted on the ground. He pulled his hat from his head and sat it down next to him. What he wouldn't give to be next to her to see her smile.

"Are you free tonight?" he asked. He had the perfect place for them to go. Somewhere they could release tension, have fun, and laugh. Then he'd take her out for a good meal.

"Tonight?" She paused. "Yeah, I can work you in on my schedule. What time are you talking?"

He glanced down at his phone and took in the time. It was midday, and he'd been at work since before the sun had risen. Ranching made for long days, but seeing her after work would make it all better.

"I can be at your house by five," he said. That would give him time to leave, go home, and shower. He wouldn't dare show up at her house smelling like horse and cow manure. "And dress casual. We might get to sweating with what I have in mind."

⁂

Nykee hung up the phone and stared at it. She grinned and fell back on the couch pillows. She had been worried that Karl had changed his mind about her. It had been two days since they had seen each other, and she had been anxious, waiting for him to call.

That kiss had been out of this world, and when he hadn't by Saturday, she had begun to think that maybe what she'd experienced was one-sided.

But no, that couldn't be it.

She had felt the large bulge pressing against her stomach.

He was interested.

Hell, so was she.

But she'd refused to phone him first. They had exchanged numbers, but there was no way in hell was she reaching out first. She had to have some pride. If he hadn't reached out to her, she would have been bummed.

This was the first guy she was truly interested in since moving back to Shady Springs. There had been others she'd dated a few times, but none of them had done anything for her.

Dress casual. We might get to sweating with what I have in mind.

Oh God. What did that mean?

It had been so long since she'd felt the touch of a man that Karl's words had her thinking X-rated thoughts.

She wouldn't mind at all getting sweaty with that man.

He was all muscle and had practically kissed the soul from her body.

She sat up suddenly.

She would need to go shopping. She had clothes she could wear, but her undergarments were more for comfort. One thing that hadn't been on her mind when she'd got out of prison was buying lingerie.

She snatched up her phone and immediately called her sister.

"Hey, sis," Bashara's voice came on the line.

"Thank God you answered," Nykee breathed. She folded her legs underneath her and rested back on the couch.

"What's wrong?" Her sister instantly went on alert.

The relationship between siblings had strengthened ever since she had been sent away. Her siblings and parents had never left her side, nor did they ever forget about her. Nykee's darkest hours had come, and they were right there with her. She remembered the day she was being sentenced that her family was there. They had been every step of the way.

Once she'd been released, they'd ensured she had everything she would need to get back on her feet. Nykee didn't deserve the loving family she was blessed with. She had put them through hell when she was a teenager.

"I might have a date," she announced.

Her sister's squeal burst through the phone. She had to remove it from her ear to save her eardrum.

"Really? I'm so happy for you. Then what is the problem?"

"Shara, I haven't gone on a real date in like a year and a half." She groaned.

Three dates. That's all she'd done since she'd got out of prison. One guy had a thing for prison women. She'd nipped that in the bud. She wasn't going to be a kink or fantasy for some creep. Another one had practically sprinted when she did tell him that she had been in prison. There might have been scuff marks left on the floor with as fast as he had run from her. The third guy had been some gaming nerd that she had met online. That ended her bout on finding love through matching sites.

"And you really like this guy?" Shara's voice lowered. The background noise faded, meaning her sister must have moved to another room in her home. With three kids and a husband, there was never a dull moment in her household.

"I do. He's so damn fine, funny, and he works on the Blazing Eagle Ranch." Nykee sighed. She played with the bottom of her shirt.

"Where did you two meet?"

"He came and dropped off his mother's dog for her appointment." Nykee smiled. He had looked so out of place in What the Fluff that it was comical. A big strong ranch hand dropping off his mother's Frenchie. She sighed. If he did favors like that for his mother, that meant he was a good man.

"Sounds like a winner in my book. Cute, obviously made you laugh, does things for his mother, and has a good job—sis, you better claim him." Shara laughed.

"Well, that's what I'm worried about." She grimaced. Everything about him was too good to be true. Or at least for her he was.

"What are talking about?" her sister snapped.

"I mean, he's him and I'm me," she said softly.

"Oh, don't start that, Nykee." Her sister's voice hardened. "I don't want to hear that you aren't good enough for anyone."

"I'm not saying I'm not good enough." She paused. She blew out a deep breath.

Her sister wouldn't truly understand where she was coming from. Her and her husband, Rick, had a fairy-tale meeting, courting and marriage. She hated to think that she'd missed her sister's wedding because she'd been locked up. The pictures were gorgeous, and Shara deserved all of it.

"But he's going to find out that I'm an ex-con. You know how some guys act when they hear that."

"And if he runs away or doesn't want to date you anymore, then that's fine. He would have showed his true self, and you don't have time for that." Shara's voice softened. "You are an amazing woman, you had a rocky start, but now look at you. A beautiful woman with a successful business. Any man would be lucky to have you."

"Karl is different," she admitted. She thought of his determination to get her to come out with him and his friends. He hadn't hidden the fact that he'd read through her tough demeanor and picked up that she had been hurt in the past. She might as well have had a sign on her forehead. She had thought she was good at hiding her feelings, but he saw straight through her.

"Different in what way?"

"I mean that he's into me," she joked. Had he hit his head or something? Was a guy like Karl truly into her?

"Ha, ha. Very funny, sis." Shara gave a dry chuckle. "Okay, so you like him, and he likes you. What's the problem?"

"We're going out today when he gets off work, and I don't have anything to um, wear." There, she hoped her sister got what she was trying to say.

"As in clothing?"

"You know what I mean!" Nykee laughed.

"Oh, you mean the sexy undies..." Shara giggled. "So you really must like him if you are thinking about those."

"I mean, I'm going to try not to throw myself at him, but if the offer is out there, let's just say I'm jumping on it." She fell into a fit of laughter with her sister. They usually shared everything with each other, and there was never any judgement between the two of them.

"Okay, okay. I believe that store Lace and Dreams is still there. Why don't you go there and pick up a few things?"

Nykee put her sister on speakerphone and brought up the internet on her phone. She typed in the name of the store and was immediately taken to their website.

It was just the kind of store she would need.

"You are a lifesaver, sis." She glanced at the time and saw the store had just opened. She would have plenty of time to grab a few things, come home, shower, and primp herself. She wasn't sure where the night would lead, but she was open to anything.

"You need to take a picture of this guy. I need to see him. We won't be back in town for another few weeks."

"I'm sure I can do that." She jumped off the couch and flew into her room to throw on some clothes. "I got to go. Call you later. Love you!"

"Love you, too, sis. Good luck, and call me tomorrow with all the details!"

"Well, I'm hoping there will be something good to share." She hung up the phone and tossed it on the bed. She closed her eyes briefly and exhaled. Today was going to be a new beginning. Shara was right. She would be honest with Karl tonight about her time away, and if he was no longer interested in her, then his loss.

❦   6   ❦

ykee parked her car in front of Lace and Dreams. How had she never known about this place?

Oh, yeah. She hadn't been interested in giving up the cookie to anyone, so why would she need sexy underwear? Most of her undergarments were for comfort only.

Not that she was opposed to wearing matching bras and panties.

She just hadn't had any motivation to purchase any until today.

Nykee exited her vehicle and went inside. She was immediately hit with a wonderful scent of fresh flowers. She glanced around, and it was a woman's dream shop. The name truly fit the atmosphere.

She browsed around and took in the store. There

were several women shopping. Two were blushing and whispering loudly about a pair of crotchless panties one was holding.

Nykee smiled and shook her head.

"Can I help you?" a voice said behind her.

Nykee spun around and froze in place. She recognized the woman as someone who'd grown up on the same street she had.

"Hey, Lindsey." Nykee's smile faded.

"Nykee." Lindsey eyed her warily. The expression on her face was one that Nykee had become used to ever since she'd moved back to town. Lindsey and her family lived across the street from Nykee and her family. "Is there something I can help you find?"

"I'm browsing. Time to buy some new bras." She sniffed. She reached up and held on to the strap of her purse and stood tall. She wasn't going to let Lindsey's judging eyes kill her mood. She had a right to shop here just like every other woman who walked around.

"I can help you." Lindsey's mouth tightened into a line, and she waved a hand for Nykee to follow her. Lindsey was tall with blonde hair that rested on her shoulders. Her black dress was form-fitting, and her legs appeared a mile long with her high heels.

Nykee followed behind her over to a few racks where there were pretty garments hanging.

"Take a look around and let me know if you would like to try anything on," Lindsey said. She offered a fake smile.

"Sure, I'll do that." Nykee focused on the items around her. She went on and ignored Lindsey while she shopped. She didn't care what the woman thought of her. She was sure Lindsey had her assumptions about her, and they wouldn't be anything she hadn't heard before.

Nykee knew who she was and that she had the money to afford the items she was interested in. She had worked hard to get her business off the ground, and it was successful.

She held a few cute bras and the matching panties in her hands. She wouldn't call Lindsey over until she was ready to try them on. Without looking, she knew Lindsey was watching her.

She could watch all she wanted. Nykee wasn't doing anything wrong.

"Finding everything okay?" Another voice sounded beside Nykee.

She turned and found one of the other saleswomen standing next to her. This one wore a name label marked 'Steph.'

"Yes, I'm ready to try these on." Nykee held up the items.

"Oh, sure, I can help you. Has anyone offered to measure you?" Steph asked.

"No, they didn't." Nykee glanced over Steph's shoulder and found Lindsey scowling at her. She rolled her eyes and focused back on Steph. "Would you mind helping me?"

"Of course." Steph broke out into a genuine smile and waved for Nykee to follow her. "Was anyone helping you?"

"Nope." Nykee hoped the women worked off commission. She didn't want Lindsey getting anything from her.

Steph escorted her into a fitting room and took the items from her and hung them up. She whipped out a measuring tape and within minutes had Nykee measured.

"I'm going to run out and get the correct sizes for you. Be right back." Steph scurried away and disappeared back into the store.

Nykee walked back into the small changing stall and blew out a deep breath. She was excited about her upcoming purchase. Footsteps echoed outside the stall. She opened the door and found Lindsey standing there.

"What do you want?" Nykee asked. She rested her hands on her waist. She didn't care that she didn't have a top on. Whatever Lindsey had to say, she was ready for her.

"Coming in here to make sure nothing gets misplaced." Lindsey shrugged nonchalantly.

"What is that supposed to mean?" Nykee narrowed her eyes on Lindsey. She took a step toward the blonde and paused.

"Nothing. Doing my job and making sure the changing rooms are neat and tidy." Lindsey tilted her head to the side.

It took everything Nykee had to stay rooted in her spot.

"And you're outside my stall because?" Nykee raised her eyebrow up in a dare. She wanted her to admit she was checking to make sure Nykee wasn't stealing. Prison had definitely taught her one thing.

How to defend herself.

"Okay, I'm back." Steph breezed back into the changing area. She was holding bras in Nykee's correct size. She paused and looked between the two of them before focusing on Lindsey. "Did she call for assistance?"

"No, she didn't. I came to clean out the room," Lindsey lied.

"But I did that before I brought this nice young lady back here," Steph said, catching her in a lie.

Nykee glanced at her and couldn't help the smirk that appeared on her lips.

"Oh, I didn't know that." Lindsey scoffed. She tossed her blonde hair over her shoulder and marched out of the room.

"That was weird," Steph murmured. She smiled and motioned to Nykee to go back into her little changing stall. "Here are these in the correct sizes. Let me know when you are ready."

"Yes, ma'am." Nykee took the items and went back into her room. She made a mental note to tip Steph really well. Each item Steph brought her was amazing and fit well. Nykee stared at herself in the mirror and couldn't believe who stared back at her.

Someone who was sexy.

That would never have been a word she would have used to describe herself. Her curves were high-lighted, her tattoos appeared softer and more femi-nine. She turned around and bit back a laugh—the lace did nothing to hide her ample behind the Lord had blessed her with.

She grew excited.

"Seriously," she uttered underneath her breath. She had just met this guy and she was already worried about sex with him.

She bit her lip, anxiety filling her. She'd only ever been with Foster. He had consumed her from her teenage years till she went away to prison. No one would have dared laid a finger on her before.

She had been his property.

Nykee blinked and focused on her image in the mirror. The room was filled with so much. She hadn't realized she and Steph had picked it all out.

She wished Shara was here with her. Her sister would know which ones she should get. After trying them all on, she put her clothes back on and left the changing room.

"Make your final decisions?" Steph smiled as she met Nykee out in the main floor.

Nykee ignored the glare that was shot her way from Lindsey.

"I'm going to take them all," she announced, holding up the large pile accumulated in her arms. She made sure that her voice was loud enough for the blonde bitch to hear her.

It would put a dent on her credit card, but that would be okay. She had never really splurged on herself before, and there was no time like the present.

"Wonderful!" Steph practically squealed. She took some of the load from Nykee and escorted her over to the counter. "I'm so glad I was able to help you find everything you wanted."

"Yes, thank you. It's been a while since I've

purchased such nice things for myself." Nykee reached inside her purse and took her wallet out.

"I'm sure it is. People like you don't get nice things when you're locked up." Lindsey sighed, walking behind Nykee.

"Come again?" Nykee whirled around and slammed her wallet on the counter. Her eyes locked on Lindsey who moved over to a table and pretended to straighten the panties on it. The store grew silent as all eyes turned toward them. Nykee dropped her purse next to her wallet and took a step toward Lindsey.

"She didn't say anything!" Steph flew around the counter and moved between Nykee and Lindsey.

Nykee's gaze didn't move off Lindsey's tall frame. The woman didn't know what she was getting into, but Nykee was only too ready to give her a little taste. She knew the kind of family Lindsey came from. They turned their noses up at anyone who wasn't like them. Lindsey and her sister were perfect in everyone's eyes.

"She did, and I want her to say it again to my face," Nykee bit out between clenched teeth. Her hands balled into tight little fists. There was one thing she did learn in prison, and that was to defend herself.

"Lindsey, go take out the trash," Steph ordered.

She shot a glare at Lindsey who stood tall and brushed her hands along her dress.

"Sure," she said. Her chin tilted up in the air before she turned and stalked away.

The other patrons in the shop had paused and nervously looked around.

"Please, return to your browsing," Steph said, giving a nervous chuckle. She pressed on a small button to the earpiece she had on. "Carol, can you come out to the showroom and assist some of the clients, please."

Nykee spun around and moved back to the counter. She had to get herself together. She couldn't let people like Lindsey get to her. Falling back into that dark place wasn't healthy for her.

Nykee had been an emotional mess when she had been released from prison. The only thing that calmed her and made her feel good about herself was working with animals.

Steph came to stand next to Nykee. She rested a hand on her forearm. "Are you all right, Miss Nash?"

"Yeah, I'm just fine." Nykee jerked her head in a nod. Out of the corner of her eye, she saw an older woman appear and began walking around offering to assist the other patrons.

"Let me get you checked out." Steph moved back

around the counter and began ringing Nykee's items out.

Nykee inhaled and slowly let the air out. Her heart rate gradually calmed down.

Lindsey would not ruin her day.

The last thing she needed was for someone to call the sheriff's department because she'd dragged Lindsey by her hair through the store.

Nykee straightened and stood to her full height. She wasn't ashamed of having gone to prison. She glanced around, and no one was staring at her anymore.

"I do have to apologize for Lindsey. I'm not sure what got in to her. That is not how we treat customers here. I'm going to give you a coupon for the trouble," Steph said. She held a worried look on her face.

"I appreciate it, but if you can't already tell, Lindsey and I know each other personally," Nykee admitted.

"It still didn't give her the right to say such mean things." Steph finished ringing her up and tallied the total.

It was astounding, but Nykee didn't care.

She had worked hard to get to where she was.

Nykee handed over her credit card and hefted her purse back onto her shoulder. She watched Steph carefully package her purchase into three large bags that were pink and black with the store's logo on it.

"Thank you for all of your help," Nykee murmured. She slid her card back into her wallet and dropped it into her purse. She took the bags from Steph and was finally able to smile.

"Please make sure you come back. I'd love to help you with anything else you're searching for." Steph offered her a genuine smile.

Nykee exited the store and breathed in a sigh of relief. The fresh air calmed the rest of her nerves. She glanced across the street and saw the Shady Bean Café. She'd heard they had good coffee, and right now she could go for a strong cup.

Nykee arrived at her car and moved to the trunk. She'd put her bags away, grab a cup of coffee, then check out the other shops in the area.

The hairs on the back of her neck rose. The wheels of an approaching vehicle sounded behind her. It paused, the brakes giving a slight squeak. Looking over her shoulder, she froze.

A sheriff's cruiser.

Slamming the trunk shut, she turned around and watched the driver's window roll down.

"Mornin' there," a deep voice called out. Deputy Pittman eyed her before giving her a nod.

"Good morning," she replied dryly. Nykee was no

stranger to the sheriff's department showing themselves around town. She tried to not take offense that they always wanted to ensure she knew they were around anywhere she went.

Hell, she wouldn't be surprised if the bitch Lindsey had called them on her.

But she had done no wrong, so there wouldn't be any reason for them to stop her.

"Can I speak with you for a moment?" Deputy Pittman opened the door and stepped out.

Her gut clenched.

She breathed a slow breath and remained calm. "Sure. I have a few moments."

"Were you about to leave?" he asked, motioning to her car. He gave the false sense that he was trying to make small talk, but Nykee still had her street smarts and could scent the bullshit a mile away. "Beautiful day, isn't it."

"It is, and no, I wasn't." She kept her reply short and curt.

"What do you have planned for the day?" he asked.

"Is there a reason why you're asking me this?" she asked. She tilted her head to the side and met his gaze full-on. He wasn't going to intimidate her. She had done no wrong and was enjoying the day. While in prison, she had learned her rights. She wasn't the young stupid girl from the past. She had taken that time she was away to educate herself.

"Just making friendly conversation." He shrugged. He tugged on his hat and focused his attention on her.

"But we're not friends," she replied bluntly. She hefted the strap of her purse on her shoulder and turned to walk away. "Am I being detained?

She threw this question at him. It was something she had learned that all lawmen had to answer. If he wasn't detaining her, then she had the right to leave. If he was, then she knew what to do next. Her muscles tightened as she waited for him to answer.

"No."

"Well, you have a wonderful day."

"Now hold on." The tone in his voice changed.

She glanced at him and waited.

He rested his hand on his utility belt and faced her fully. "There have been string of robberies lately."

"Am I being detained?" she asked again, and this time her voice was firm.

"No, you are not." He glared at her.

He was looking for a reason to take her in. She could feel it.

But it wouldn't be today or any other day. She'd done no wrong.

"As I was saying, you have a good day, sir." She

spun around and stalked away. Whatever he was investigating had nothing to do with her, and she didn't want to involve herself at all. Nykee was no longer the naïve girl of her youth, following the crowd. He had no right to detain or question her. She blew out a deep breath and jogged across the street.

She was not going to let them ruin her day.

Nykee arrived at the Shady Bean Café, and once the scent of the establishment hit her, she immediately decided she was indulging in a pastry with her coffee.

$$\text{❦} \quad 7 \quad \text{❦}$$

Karl turned onto Nykee's street. He wiped his hands on his jeans and barked a laugh. He couldn't remember the last time he'd been nervous when picking up a woman.

Those day were long gone.

He'd been a teenager the last time he could remember.

There was something about Nykee where he wanted to make sure this date was perfect. He had something crazy lined up for them. It wasn't going to be the typical date where he took her to the movies and dinner.

They would do dinner, because he would love to sit down with her and learn all about her.

She looked as if she loved adventure, and what he

had planned for them would definitely get their hearts thumping.

He pulled into the driveway of a little cottage home. It looked perfect for Nykee. The only thing it was missing was the white picket fence.

Karl cut the engine and sat back. His heart was racing. He'd flown home after work and jumped right in the shower. He hadn't wanted to be late.

He would also admit that he couldn't wait to see her. Their telephone conversation replayed in his head constantly.

Hell, his dick got hard even thinking of her flirting with him over the phone.

He opened the door and walked around the truck. He jogged up the couple of stairs and hit the doorbell. He ran a hand along his chin and grimaced. He should have shaved, but it would have taken a little longer. He was anxious to see her.

Footsteps sounded, and within seconds the door opened and there she stood.

"Hey." Karl cleared his throat. The moment their eyes met, a lump formed in his throat to keep him from speaking.

His gaze moved down Nykee's form, and he was captivated.

"Hi yourself," she murmured. Her big brown eyes grew even larger as they watched him.

She was dressed in skin-tight jeans, a red blouse that showcased her forearms. He made a mental note to get close enough to see what was inked on her arms. She had on light makeup, and her hair was held back in a ponytail. Her small feet were encased in black flats.

"I hope this is casual enough, or do I need to go and change?" she asked.

"No, you're fine. Beautiful." He scratched his head. He held the door open and stepped back.

"Oh good. I was worried when you said we may sweat." She reached over and snagged her purse and threw it across her body. She stepped out of the house on the small landing and closed and locked the door.

"What you have on is perfect for what I have planned." He grinned. He stepped down the stairs and waited for her.

She turned around, and he offered his hand to her. A shy smile ghosted her lips as she slid hers into his larger one.

"You, Mr. Tanis, are such a gentleman." She giggled.

His dick jerked at the sound of her laugh. His smile widened. He tugged her along toward the truck. "You have met my mother already so you should know she wouldn't raise my brother and I no other way."

He opened the door for her and assisted her into the pickup.

"Well, I will have to thank her." Her lips curled into a true smile, and Karl froze in place.

Her face lit up, and it was the most gorgeous expression he'd ever seen. He made a promise that he would do whatever he needed to do to ensure this woman continued to smile like that for him.

He didn't care about anyone else as long as he was the only one who got her true smiles.

"What is it?" She paused.

Her little head tilt was so damn cute, he ached to kiss her.

But if he kissed her, he couldn't promise they would actually leave and go where he had planned for them to spend some time.

"You're really beautiful," he replied honestly. He cupped her cheek, needing to touch her.

"Thank you." She reached up and covered his hand. A slight twinkle entered her eyes. "Are we going to stand here all night and stare at each other?"

He blinked and barked a laugh.

"Nope." He stepped back and shut the door. He jogged around the vehicle and hopped into the driver's seat. He slid his safety belt on and hit the button to start the engine. "You haven't eaten, have you?"

"Earlier when I went shopping. I stopped at the Shady Bean Café."

He backed the truck out of her driveway and guided them onto the road.

"How'd you like it?" he asked.

It was a locally owned café owned by Nasia. He'd been there a few times and now he saw how Nasia was able to snag Stan. The food was really good.

Karl turned on the radio. He found a light rock channel and left it there and lowered the volume so they would be able to converse without yelling.

"I loved it. I hadn't been there yet, but I really liked it. I would definitely go back, and they had this strawberry concoction that was to die for. I'm sure it went straight to my hips." She laughed.

"I've been there before, too. My coworker's girl, Nasia, owns the place. She does a monthly thing where she always adds something new to the menu. Stan has brought a few things out to the ranch to let us try."

Everyone on the ranch always lived for the day when Stan brought out the white boxes from his truck. Apparently, Nasia wanted to experiment on cowboys with her recipes, and no one objected.

"Well, you can pass on that she has a new faithful customer," Nykee said.

"You wouldn't be the first." He laughed.

"So what do you have planned for us?" Nykee leveled him with her gaze.

He tightened his grip on the steering wheel to keep from reaching for her.

"How's your throwing arm?" he asked, peeking over at her.

"Huh?"

"You know. Your arm. How are you at throwing stuff?" he asked.

"Not sure. I was never one to play sports." She had a quizzical expression on her face.

"Don't worry, I'll teach you what you need to know." He slid a hand across the console and took hers in his. He couldn't help it. He just had to touch her.

"And we are going...?" She drew out her words.

"Ax throwing." He grinned and entwined their fingers.

Nykee's eyebrows jerked up high.

"Ax throwing?"

"You know, where you take an ax and throw it at a bull's eye? It's fun. Tell me you've been before."

"Can't say I have." She shook her head.

He didn't miss how she covered their hands with her other one.

"Where have you been?" he joked.

She faced the window, but it wasn't before he saw her smile fade. He squeezed her again, unsure what had just transpired.

"Don't worry. You are in good hands."

She chuckled at his joke. They drove in a comfortable silence as he guided them through the town. Shady Springs had blossomed in the last few years. More people were moving to the booming town. Housing developments were going up, and the farming and ranching businesses were doing phenomenally.

He loved the area and wouldn't mind settling there forever. He had an amazing job and owned his own home. Shady Springs was a family town that was safe and a great place to raise kids. He'd heard Parker mention that the school system was top-notch.

All he needed was a good woman he wouldn't mind spending the rest of his life with, two-point-five children, a few animals to round out the perfect family.

"Can I ask you a question?" she asked.

"Of course."

"What's up with you always wanting to hold my

hand?" She focused those beautiful brown eyes on him before dropping her gaze to their joined hands.

He gave a shrug and flipped on the turning signal. He slowed the vehicle down, waiting for traffic to pass.

"I like how small they are compared to mine," he began. He used his one hand to turn the vehicle onto the long road. They were almost to the place, but he wasn't in any rush to get there.

"Really? So if I had hands the same size as yours, you wouldn't hold them?"

He broke out into a fit of laughter. He glanced over at her to see her smile had returned.

He liked this Nykee. Already she was opening to him more, and he was enjoying seeing her personality break through.

"I mean, it may be a little awkward, but I still would take you out," he admitted.

"Sure you would." She gave an unladylike snort.

She made small circles with her nail on his hand. The slight movement sent a wave a desire shooting through him. His cock thickened, pressing against his jeans. He inhaled and caught a whiff of her perfume.

Everything about Nykee was turning him on.

"I would."

"Okay. What's another reason you constantly hold my hand?"

"I like you. A lot, and I want to make sure you know I'm interested." The smile slipped from his lips. This he was dead serious about and wanted to make sure that she knew he was definitely into her.

"Is that so?"

Her hand stroked the back of his, and the sensation was driving him insane. He cleared his throat and glanced over at her.

"That's nice to know," she said. "I like you, too."

"You allow me to hold your hand. Why do you let me?" He flipped the question back on her. Since she was curious about something as small as hand-holding, he was interested in her thought process.

"I like the feeling of your hand against mine. While mine is soft and small as you noted, yours are large and calloused. These are the hands of a man who isn't afraid to work with them," she murmured.

His gaze cut to hers briefly before returning to the road. Her slow, sensual caresses followed the pattern of his veins and tendons.

A few cars were headed in the same direction. The place was about a mile away and located on the outskirts of town. Trees and open land surrounded the two-lane road.

"Is that all?" His voice dropped down low.

"There's more," she quipped. Her hand resting in his tightened her grip on him. "For some strange reason, something as simple as you holding my hand makes me feel safe."

Something passed in her gaze. It was fleeting, and he didn't know what it was. There was something in her past that she was hinting at. Karl would allow her to come to him when she was ready.

He had promised he was going to move slow with her. She was one hell of a woman, and he didn't want to risk messing anything up with her.

He brought her hand to his mouth and dropped a kiss to the back of it.

"Of course. I'd never hurt you or allow anyone to." The light conversation suddenly got serious. Had someone hurt her? Put their hands on her? He wasn't sure, but he'd be damned if anything was to happen to her while he was around.

They rode the rest of the way in silence. She didn't let his hand go until they pulled into the parking lot. He killed the engine and turned to her.

"Ready to go get destructive?" he asked.

"I am."

He shot her a wink and exited the vehicle. The parking lot was filled with plenty of trucks and cars. Chuck It was a popular place to hang out. He tried to inconspicuously adjust himself. His relaxed jeans were suddenly two sizes too small thanks to his erect cock. He arrived at Nykee's door and opened it.

He held out his hand and assisted her down.

He bit back a groan when her soft, curvy body slid along his. She stood before him with her head tilted back. Her lips parted as they stared at each other.

He couldn't resist taking a taste of her lips.

Karl cupped her face in his while he angled his head to the side. Her lips parted, granting his tongue entrance to her mouth. She tasted of peppermints and sunshine.

She pressed close to him, a moan slipping from her. Her hands rested on his forearms as she rose on her tiptoes.

Laughter off in the distance reminded him that they were in a very public parking lot. As much as he wanted to strip her clothes off and push her against the side of his truck so he could sink into her, he held back. Their date did not need to end with the police being called.

He backed away slightly, their lips still touching. He rested his forehead on hers and he tried to catch his breath.

"Jesus, I can't keep my hands to myself," he muttered.

She opened her eyes and smiled at him. "Well, good thing I don't want you to."

What little air was left in his lungs was ripped out.

Hot damn.

Karl stared down at her, speechless.

"Let's go have some fun, little lady." His grinned widened, and he took her by the hand again. He pulled her forward and shut the door to his truck.

Tonight was getting better by the minute.

❃   8   ❃

"Why won't mine hit the target?" Nykee stomped her foot.

She watched the kid a few stalls away swing and toss his ax. He appeared about thirteen, and his ax landed dead center of his target.

She pouted and folded her arms in front of her.

"All right, little lady. Let me show you again." Karl's arms wrapped around her from behind.

She couldn't help but lean back in his embrace. He had been right to bring her here. It was so much fun. She hadn't laughed this hard in a long while.

A shiver rippled through her.

She had prepared for their date night. The longer she was around him, the more she wanted to grab him by the hand and tell him to drive back to her house so she could have her wicked way with him.

His attention had been on her the entire night. There were a group of a women located on the other end of their row of stalls that kept trying to catch Karl's attention, but he paid them no mind.

He only had eyes for her.

It made her feel good and womanly.

Foster hadn't had any issues with openly looking at other women when she'd been with him. He'd cheated on her constantly, and in the life they'd lived, she had gotten used to it.

She shivered again. Without a doubt there was no comparing Karl to Foster.

Foster was a man whore, a gangster who didn't have any problems risking her life or safety to get what he wanted. It was Foster who had her stealing and doing drug deals to save his own hide. He hadn't cared about her.

There were plenty of times he'd told her he loved her.

The young, naïve Nykee had fallen for it, too.

Karl, on the other hand, was a good man. He worked hard, came from a respectable family, and he was into her.

She rested her hands on his and looked up over her shoulder at him.

"I'm a lost cause," she muttered. Her axes had

come close to the center, but she hadn't been lucky enough to hit it yet.

"Come on." He nudged her forward toward their stall.

She bit back a moan at the feeling of his hardened body pressed against hers. His warmth radiated through his clothes, and she didn't miss the bulge in his jeans that brushed her ass.

"What you need to do is center yourself with the target," he said.

He moved them over to where she was standing midline to their stall. Chuck It was a pretty large facility with exposed wood beams. The atmosphere was fun and light. Laughter filled the air. There were multiple groups of people having fun. Young and old were tossing axes.

"You're going to hold the ax with both hands. You're not a pro like me yet." He snickered.

She rolled her eyes. He had started showing off by throwing his axes with one hand. The cocky ranch hand hit the red center multiple times. He reached down and guided her arms up in the air.

The position may have been innocent to anyone watching, but being in the midst of it led Nykee to imagining erotic images. Holding her arms up thrust her large breasts forward, her back rested against

Karl's chest, and her ass was snuggled quite nicely with his cock.

She blinked and tried to clear the images of them in the same position with him naked and pulling her hair so her head rested back on his shoulder.

"Keep your eyes on the target. You can't throw an ax with your eyes closed." Karl's warm breath skated along her ear.

His deep voice sent chills down her spine. She blinked and opened her eyes, not realizing she'd closed them.

"Okay," she breathed.

Oh God.

How was she going to make it through their entire date? She wondered what he'd think if she said, "Fuck dinner, let's go back to my place?"

"Keep your eye on the red target, then toss the ax." He moved their arms and acted as if she were throwing.

He stepped away from her and motioned to her ax on the ledge.

She instantly missed the feeling of him. She nodded and reached for her ax. She did as he'd said. Made sure she was lined up exactly with the target. Lifted the ax, holding the handle with both hands, and kept her eye on the prize.

She tossed it and held her breath.

The blue-handled weapon flew through the air and slammed into the red circle on the wooden target.

A scream erupted from her.

Her first bull's eye. She turned and hopped into Karl's arms. Somehow her legs managed to wrap around his waist in her excitement.

"I did it!" she screamed.

He laughed and held her in his arms.

"You did." He grinned, holding her by her ass.

She cupped his cheeks and pressed a hard kiss to his lips before wiggling out of his arms. Nykee honestly didn't know how she'd landed in his arms. He didn't even act as if her one-hundred-and-eighty-five-pound frame bothered him. She slid down him and had to keep her arms around him. Her knees suddenly went weak when he tilted her chin up and dropped another kiss to her lips.

She blinked and shyly met his gaze.

"What was that one for?" she asked.

"Just because," he murmured.

He kissed her again, this time on her forehead, and she had to bite back a whimper.

Karl Tanis had better be careful.

"You going to take another turn?" she asked.

He walked to their target and pulled the ax free

from the wood. He sauntered back to her, his heated gaze roaming her body.

Every time he looked at her like that, she was surprised her clothes didn't go up in flames.

"That depends." He gave a shrug and arrived back at her side.

"On what?" she asked.

He rested the ax on the ledge and took her hand in his. "On if you worked up an appetite or not."

His lips slid into his sexy grin of his that had her heart fluttering.

"Oh, I most certainly have," she breathed.

His eyes darkened, and she knew he understood her.

"Well, good. I have the perfect place for us to pick up something to eat." He tugged her in close to his body and wrapped his arm around her shoulder.

"Where are we going now?" she asked. Nykee was having fun, and honestly, she didn't want the night to end. After all of their fun and games, her stomach was reminding her that it was empty.

"I hope you like barbecue," Karl said.

Her stomach growled again. "I love barbecue."

The man was definitely after her heart. They walked through Chuck It and headed out. Nykee had fun and was glad Karl had thought of this place. It was her first time doing something like this. It had been a long time since she had been able to relax all the way and just enjoy herself.

They exited the building, and the sun had gone down. The dark sky twinkled with the millions of tiny stars that were painted along the canvas. Nykee leaned into Karl and placed her arm around his waist.

This was nice.

They arrived at the truck, and she paused by the door. She moved to stand in front of Karl and stared up at him.

"Thank you," she said.

He automatically moved in closer, closing the gap between them. He reached up and brushed the few strands of her hair away from her face that had escaped her ponytail.

"Anytime, beautiful. I love hearing and seeing you laugh." He trailed a finger along her temple and down her cheek.

"It actually felt good to relax and not worry about anything," she admitted.

"I don't know what's in your past that haunts you, but I'm here to wipe the darkness away from you."

Nykee's heart skipped a beat. She rested her hands on his chest and rose on her toes. He met her and covered her mouth with his.

She'd never had anyone who made her feel the

way she did with Karl. Their lips molded together in a passionate, deep kiss.

Nykee slid her hands up his hardened chest and entwined them together at the base of his neck. She held on for dear life as he controlled the kiss.

He took his time, sweeping his tongue into her mouth. It was if a new breath of fresh air had blown into Nykee. She had thought she was living once she was released from prison, but now she saw she hadn't been living, she had just been existing.

In the few hours she'd spent with Karl so far, she wanted more out of life. She wanted happiness. She wanted what her parents and siblings had with their spouses.

Was she hoping for too much at the moment?

Honestly, she didn't care.

She was going to enjoy the time she had with Karl and take everything one step at a time and see where it led.

Hopefully, the night would end with the both of them naked and their bodies entangled together.

Karl pulled away and laughed.

"I swear I mean to feed you," he muttered. He grinned and brushed her bottom lip with his finger. "But again, I can't keep my hands off you."

Her stomach chose that moment to make itself

known. They shared a laugh. She rested her forehead on his chest, embarrassed.

"Oh, goodness," she groaned.

"Come on, woman. I can't have you passing out from starvation."

He assisted her into the truck and shut the door. She watched him walk around the hood of the vehicle. She touched her lips and found them swollen from his kisses. He hopped into the driver's seat and smiled at her.

He started the engine and took her hand in his.

She glanced down at their entwined fingers.

This was what a true relationship must feel like. She felt all giddy inside and was unfamiliar with this feeling.

One thing she did know was that she didn't want it to go away.

❧

"OH MY GOD, THIS IS SO GOOD." NYKEE GROANED.

Karl watched her lick the barbecue sauce from her fingers. She laughed and reached for a napkin.

There was new barbecue place, and Karl had been wanting to try it out. He'd heard great things about it. The restaurant was a to-go-only place. They had runners who brought out the food once you'd ordered it. Once they had grabbed their food, Karl had driven them to a park where they could stargaze afterwards.

He had wanted to end the night well and thought it would be fun to lie back and stare at the stars.

"I'm glad you liked it. I had been hearing good things about this place." He finished off the rib he had been working on and tossed the bone over the side of the truck.

Once they'd arrived at the park, he'd opened the tailgate and laid out a blanket he kept in the back. They had spread their food out on the platters they came on and dove in. He liked how Nykee wasn't shy about eating. The little sighs and moans when she tried something new had him captivated.

"The meat is falling off the bone." She held up her rib, and the meat practically fell into her waiting hand. She popped the morsel into her mouth and groaned. She shook her head and waved to the food. "This was a great idea."

"I aim to please." He tossed her a wink. He glanced down at his watch and took in the time. It was getting late, and the moon was high. The stars were twinkling bright as if telling him they were ready for them.

"Well, you are doing a fantastic job," she said.

Nykee reached over and snagged on of the wet napkins to clean off her hands.

"Good." He chuckled.

He finished off the last of the baked beans in his container and replaced the lid on the bowl. They worked together in silence and cleaned up their mess. He stored the containers that still had food in the paper bag that the restaurant provided.

"You can take the leftovers home."

"Are you sure? Maybe we can split them," she offered.

"I don't mind. You can have them." He took the empty containers and put them in the other bag. He jumped down from the truck and walked over to the trash can that was near their parking spot.

A lot of people came up here to gaze or sneak away for alone time. It was frequented by the public and closed around one in the morning. So far there was only one other car that he could see.

He walked back and caught sight of lights coming up the road that led to the parking lot. From what he could see it appeared to be a police cruiser. He made it back to the truck where Nykee sat on the edge of the gate and swung her legs back and forth.

"Ready for the show?" he asked.

He stopped in front of her. She spread her legs to

allow him to stand between them. He rested his hands beside her hips, entrapping her.

He pressed a soft kiss to her lips.

Karl had a hard time keeping his hands and lips off her.

"Well, it depends. What type of show are we talking about?" she asked. A sassy grin appeared on her face.

"I was talking about the stars, but I'm sure I can arrange another one more private for you if you would like." He leaned down and captured her lips again.

"That we would definitely have to arrange," she murmured, her lips brushing his. She reached up and caressed the side of his face.

"Yes, ma'am." He grinned.

"Hello there, folks," a voice called out.

Karl turned and saw the police cruiser parked in front of his truck. He had backed into the parking spot so they would be able to sit in the back and look up at the sky.

"Evening," Karl called out.

Nykee turned around and glanced at the newcomer. Her muscles tensed, and she grew quiet.

Deputy Griffen walked toward them.

"I thought this was your truck, Karl. How's everything going?" The deputy drew closer to them.

Nykee stared down at her folded hands. Karl didn't miss how her demeanor changed when the deputy approached them.

"Everything's going great. Going to do a little stargazing for a bit before heading out of here," Karl said.

The deputy's attention was on Nykee. The hairs on the back of Karl's neck rose. He didn't like how the deputy looked at her.

"Well, howdy there, Nykee Nash," Deputy Griffen said.

"Deputy Griffen." Nykee sniffed.

"Fancy seeing you here. Didn't know you were into stargazing." Griffen folded his arms in front of him.

"There's a lot of things you don't know about me, Deputy." Nykee sniffed again.

It didn't take a rocket scientist to pick up on the animosity between the two of them.

"Oh, but there is plenty I do know about you, girl." Deputy snickered.

"Is there a problem?" Karl asked. He stepped closer to Nykee and leaned against the side of his truck. He wasn't sure what was going on, but he didn't like how the deputy was treating Nykee.

"No problem at all. I just came up here to make sure everything was good. The park closes at one, so don't stay too late." Griffen glanced away and scanned the area.

"Yes, sir. We won't be here too long," Karl assured him.

"Nykee, you haven't heard from any of your old friends, have you?" The deputy paused and waited for her reply.

Nykee sat still, fiddling with her fingers, and didn't look at him.

"I'm sure you've heard there's been a few issues going around town. Now we can't afford to have you and your little friends coming home and stirring up trouble. We've cleaned up this town mighty nice."

What the hell was the deputy talking about?

Nykee still didn't respond.

Griffen eyed Karl and tipped his hat to him.

"Have a good night," Griffen said. He spun around and began walking away. He paused and turned around. "And, Karl, you might want to think about the company you keep. You never really know people."

"What—"

"Leave it alone, Karl," Nykee said softly. Her voice was barely audible. Her shoulders were slumped, and she'd had a defeated expression.

Karl glanced back at where the deputy had stood, but the space was empty. The sound of the car door shutting echoed, and he watched the patrol car pull off.

Karl swung back around and moved to stand in front of Nykee. He didn't know what had just happened.

"I'm completely confused," he admitted.

She glanced up and rolled her eyes. He moved closer to her and rested his hands on her thighs. Her bottom lip quivered. She inhaled sharply and shook her head.

"I'm not sure what you've heard about me," she began. She closed her eyes briefly and exhaled sharply. "So I might as well tell you now, then you can take me home."

"What is it?"

"If you can't already tell, Deputy Griffen and I have a history. Let's just say in my younger years I wasn't a good girl. I think Griffen holds the record on arresting me the most in the sheriff's department."

Karl swallowed hard. That hadn't been what he was expecting. He kept quiet, not wanting to interrupt her.

"Okay. None of us were perfect when we were younger," he said. Hell, he and his friends had certainly got into their share of trouble.

Her gaze swung to him, and his breath lodged in his throat.

"I hung out with the wrong crowd, got caught up with a guy who didn't give a shit about me, and I've done time in prison."

"Okay." He reached up and cupped her cheek in his hand. He honestly didn't care about her past mistakes. She owned her own business, was beautiful, and was a good woman. He believed everyone deserved second and third chances in life. No one person was perfect. "So you did a little time in prison, so what?"

"Are you serious?" She stared at him as if he'd grown a second head. She brushed his hand away from her face. "You sure you haven't been working too long in the sun and may have had a heat stroke?"

"Why would you say that?" He was taken aback.

"Usually when a guy hears I'm an ex-con, they either run for the hills or they have some sick kink about women in prison." Nykee folded her arms in front of herself. She eyed him wearily.

Now he understood the darkness in her eyes and why she didn't trust many people. Those friends of hers and her former boyfriend sounded like a piece of work. They'd used her, and he was sure there was more to the story, but he wasn't going to pry. Whenever she felt ready to share with him, she would.

But it didn't take away how beautiful she was, her sparkling personality he was finally getting to see, or the woman she had become.

Whatever she had done in her past made her who she was now.

He gripped her hips and slid her toward him. Her legs widened so he could stand between them. He tipped her chin up so he could look her in her eyes.

"I'm not running away," he whispered.

Her brown eyes studied his as if searching for the truth.

"I like you. A lot. And I want to get to know more about you. I want to know what makes you smile. What makes you laugh. What makes you moan, and what makes you scream."

Her eyes grew wider. Her lips parted slightly. Karl wanted to erase every bad deed done to this woman. She didn't deserve to be continuously judged off of her past mistakes. What she did deserve was endless amounts of pleasure that he wanted to give her.

"Karl," she breathed.

"And as for kinks, I promise I have plenty of them, but none of them involve prison." He couldn't help but grin at that.

Her lips trembled slightly, and the twinkles in her eyes were returning.

"That's a good thing," she murmured.

"That I have kinks or that none of them involve a prison fantasy?" He arched an eyebrow at her.

A laugh escaped her. She leaned forward and rested her forehead on his chest. "What am I going to do with you?"

He reached down and tilted her chin back so he could meet her eyes. "Two options. One, I pull out the blanket and we stargaze like we were supposed to do." He pressed a hard kiss to her lips. He drew back slightly, his hand resting on the nape of her neck. "Or two, we can—"

"Go back to my place."

9

Karl pulled into her driveway and cut the engine. He tightened his grip on her hand and turned to face her.

"Are you sure?"

His deep voice sent a ripple of desire through her. She had expected him to run at the mention of her spending time in prison. He hadn't asked too many questions like most men did when she told them.

Not Karl.

He accepted it for what it was and moved on.

She really didn't deserve someone like him. Karl was a good man, and he saw the real her.

Having Deputy Griffen show up at the park and make his snide comments had pissed her off and was embarrassing. He'd treated her as if she were the same girl from the past. He didn't want to see that she'd changed. She had a thriving business, paid her taxes like every other citizen, and contributed to their town.

No. All he saw was the young delinquent.

But his words didn't scare Karl off. The sight of Karl stepping toward her as if to protect her from the deputy didn't go unnoticed. Karl hadn't known what was going on, but he'd sided with her.

That made a world of a difference.

"If you don't get me inside the house, I'm going to be climbing over this console to get to you," she breathed.

She didn't know where this brazen hussy came from, but that's just want Karl did to her.

Just breathing in his cologne had her tied up in knots. Her panties had already been damp, and the dark look he'd just sent her had them soaked.

He exited the vehicle without saying a word. He slid a hand through his hair, sending his strands all over the place. He opened the door and held out his hand to her. She took it and allowed him to assist her down from the oversized pickup.

Unable to resist, she reached up and brought his head down to her. Their lips met in a searing-hot kiss. She pressed closer to him. She opened her mouth to his to allow his tongue to sweep inside. Their tongues dueled together, teasing each other.

Nykee's body was on fire.

The large bulge pressing against her stomach had her core clenching. She wanted to feel that hardness pushing inside her to fill her up.

"If we don't get inside, I'm sure your neighbors won't appreciate if I take you against my truck," Karl growled.

"Right." Nykee snagged her purse from the truck and almost sprinted to her front door. She dug inside her bag to find her keys.

Karl appeared behind her, his arm wrapping around her waist to hold her to him. His lips skimmed the side of her neck while her hands shook trying to put the key into the lock. She missed again.

"Dammit."

"Here, let me." His hand encircled hers and guided the key into the hole. His warm breath bathed her ear. "I don't miss."

"Oh, please." She rolled her eyes at his silly sexual innuendo.

They turned the key, and the door unlocked. She pushed it open and walked inside with him still holding on to her. Karl pulled the key out of the lock and shut the door. He dropped them into the bowl on the table next to the door. She tossed her purse on the couch and spun back to him.

Karl leaned back against the door, and the sight

of him took her breath away. He was tall, muscular, and that damn plaid shirt was driving her crazy. It screamed cowboy, and she would have to admit she had a thing for them.

Nykee walked over to him and trapped him with her body.

"Just me and you tonight," he murmured. He reached for her and tugged her closer, closing the gap between them. He cupped her cheek, this thumb skating across her bottom lip. "No thinking or talking of the past. I want the woman standing before me."

"You have me." She exhaled. Her fingers automatically began undoing the buttons of his shirt. She was dying to see him without it.

"Do whatever you want to me."

"I plan to." She glanced up at him and grinned.

His lips spread into a wide smile. He kicked off his boots and reached for his belt.

His shirt fell open, and she pushed it off his shoulders. It fell to the floor unnoticed. She tugged on his white undershirt and pulled it over his head, leaving him bare-chested. He had a light sprinkle of hair on his chest that beelined toward his navel and disappeared underneath his jeans.

Her core clenched at the ripple of muscles and

the ridges on his abdomen. Her fingers traced each one of them.

"If I'm shirtless, you need to be, too." He gripped her shirt and tugged it over her head.

She kicked off her shoes and stood before him. His eyes darkened at the sight of her. She had chosen the black lace bra set, and from his expression, she had chosen wisely.

"Fuck."

He bent down and lifted her by the back of her knees. She wrapped her legs around him, again amazed at how easily he carried her.

She brought his face to hers and covered his lips with hers. Their kiss was hot and hard. He began walking with her and made it to the hallway. Luckily, her house was small, a two-bedroom ranch.

"Which one?" he asked.

His hands cupped her ass and kept her up high. She pointed to her door, her lips moving of their own accord. She loved the fuzz on his face. She always had a thing for men with five o'clock shadows. There was something just so sexy with the rugged look.

They burst through the door. Nykee had left the light on, unsure what time she'd arrive home and if she'd come back with company. She had cleaned her house like a madwoman earlier in the hopes that she wouldn't be alone.

Karl stopped at the bed where she slid down before him. He stood with the bed behind him. She reached for his jeans that he had unbuttoned and undid the zipper. She opened them wider and knelt on the floor.

"I can do what I want?" she asked.

"Hell yeah," he muttered.

His jeans slid down, revealing black cotton boxer briefs. His erection tented his shorts. She grinned at the size and wasn't disappointed at all. She'd felt him pressed against her so had an idea of the size.

But seeing it up close and personal had her licking her lips.

He kicked the jeans away from him while she snagged his shorts. His cock popped free, and her pussy clenched with anticipation. His cock was thick and long.

"You keep looking at my cock like that and this will be over very soon." He groaned.

She tore her gaze away from the magnificent shaft and glanced up at him. She wrapped her hand around him, surprised she was able to close her fingers around his thickness.

"Is that so?" She arched an eyebrow while running her hand along his length.

"Fuck it. Don't say I didn't warn you." He tugged

her hair free from her ponytail and entwined his fingers in her thick strands.

She ran her tongue along the underside of his shaft, getting her first taste of him. She traced all of the thick veins that lined it before reaching the mushroomed tip. She slipped it between her lips, the saltiness of his precum greeting her.

Nykee moaned, loving the taste of his essence. Her tongue swirled around the soft tip. Karl's hand tightened in her hair.

The sound of her name on his tongue increased the desire building inside her. She took her time and slipped as much of him as she could inside her mouth until he hit the back of her throat. She instinctively swallowed to keep herself from gagging. She pulled back and repeated the motion, this time stroking the base of his shaft.

His hazel eyes burned down at her. She held his gaze while she continued to suckle him. Her saliva coated him, allowing her hand to skate along the length of him easily and smoothly.

The proof of her desire for him trailed down her thighs. She needed him inside her as much as she needed to breathe.

The muscles in his abdomen trembled. He was close to spiraling out of control. The hand in her hair gripped her tightly, creating only slight pain that she welcomed.

She increased the pace, keeping her lips wrapped around him. Her free hand came up to cup his balls. She massaged them and watched intently the emotions crossing his face. His body shook, and she wanted to see him let loose. She popped him from her mouth and trailed her tongue along his shaft again. This time she moved it out of the way to lick his sac. She teased him, suckled the round orbs while her hand continued to stroke him.

He chanted her name.

She had never had a man so under her spell before.

Karl had turned all of the control over to her.

What she needed, he was giving her.

His cock seemed swell even more in her hands. Her tongue slid along the length of him, and she slipped the tip back inside her mouth.

"Nykee." Her name came out as a groan.

His hips moved softly, sending his cock farther into her mouth. She allowed him to fuck it. Her gaze drifted back up, and as soon as they met, his eyes rolled into the back of his head.

Hot ripples of his seed shot into her throat. She automatically swallowed every drop. She continued to stroke him, milking him for everything he had.

He grew still once he was done. She licked and kissed his semisoft cock. His breathing was rapid and harsh. He opened his eyes, a growl escaping from him.

"Come here."

The rest of her clothes were snatched off her and tossed to the floor. Nykee found herself on the bed with her legs spread wide and Karl's head between them.

She arched off the bed with the first lick of his tongue. The man didn't need any instructions. He captured her clit and suckled it.

A gasp tore from Nykee as the man feasted upon her. His warm hands braced against her thighs to keep them from closing. Not that she wanted to. Hell, she didn't think she get them open far enough for him.

Nykee's gasps and groans filled the air. Her hips moved, thrusting toward him while she rode his tongue.

"Karl," she cried out when he pushed a finger into her core.

Her walls were so drenched in her desire for him that his finger slid inside with little effort. He lapped up all of her juices before returning to her clit.

The man knew how to work a woman, and Nykee was grateful he was using his skills on her. He soon pressed another finger into her, stretching her out. He was a big man, and she was determined to take him fully inside her.

Nykee's fingers dove into his thick dark hair and held on for dear life. Her back arched off the bed with the electric current rippling its way through her body.

She was so close.

Never had she orgasmed this quickly with a man before.

Foster couldn't have cared less if she'd enjoyed sex with him. He would get his, and that was it. She'd learned really quick how to please herself. It was sad that most of her orgasms had come from her own hand.

But with Karl, she already saw this would be no problem. Her body responded to him with an intensity that scared her.

What if he wasn't pleased with her?

Would he tell her?

Or would he just up and leave and this be all she'd get from him?

No.

She pushed all the self-doubt away. Karl wasn't like that. She'd watched his facial expressions while she'd sucked his cock. They were all real, and with the way he was consuming her pussy at the moment, the man was thoroughly enjoying himself.

Nykee opened her eyes and glanced down and found Karl's heated gaze on her. He twirled her clit with his tongue before pulling on it. His fingers were slowly fucking her, setting a rhythm that her hips followed.

Tremors racked her body. Her breaths were coming in pants while the sensations coursing through her body alerted her that her orgasm was rushing toward her. She tightened her grip in his hair. He twisted his fingers around and pumped them inside her harder.

Nykee closed her eyes and gave in.

Her body detonated.

Her scream tore through the air. Her muscles grew tight as an overwhelming amount of pleasure washed over her. She fell back on the bed with a fine sheet of sweat coating her.

"So sweet," Karl murmured.

She opened her eyes and found him licking his fingers. Her breath caught in her throat at the erotic sight of him tasting her cream.

"Oh God," she whispered.

His eyes connected with hers. That sexy grin of his appeared on his lips. He pushed and crawled over her, bracing himself above her. His thick cock rested on her stomach, once again hard. He settled into the valley of her thighs, his length brushing her pussy.

He bent down and captured her lips in a hard, bruising kiss. The taste of her greeted her, but she didn't care. She threw herself into the kiss, pouring all of her emotions and feelings into it.

Karl dominated the kiss.

He may have let her have control at first, but now he had taken it back which she was only too willing to give to him.

He trailed hot kisses along her jawline and nuzzled his face into the crook of her neck.

Nykee rocked her hips, loving the sensation of his length teasing her.

Now if only she could get that thick cock inside her…

"Patience," he whispered in her ear. A sexy chuckle followed. He traced the lobe of her ear with his tongue. "Don't worry, I'm going to give you everything you need tonight."

Nykee whimpered.

How did this man know what she needed?

Then she thought of the orgasm he'd just pulled from her.

Oh, he knew.

He rubbed himself against her.

"You want my cock inside you?" He nipped her ear, then soothed it with his tongue.

"Yes," she hissed.

She wrapped her arms around his neck to hold him closer to her. Her breasts were mashed between them. Her hardened nipples ached against the constraints of his chest.

"Please."

"You don't have to beg me." He pressed a heated kiss to her shoulder and moved farther until he came to her breasts. His large hands encircled her mounds. She had always had full breasts, and they filled his hands perfectly. "You can have my cock. Tonight, it's yours."

She whimpered again watching him suckle her nipple into his mouth. His other hand squeezed and teased her other bud.

"Karl."

"I love the way you say my name," he breathed. He flicked her nipple with his tongue before bathing her entire mound with his tongue. He sat back on his knees and pushed her legs apart.

Karl grabbed the shaft of his hardened member. He stroked the length of his cock. Her breaths came faster as she watched him.

"Hey," he said softly.

Her eyes flicked to his.

"Eyes up here. I want you to know who's fucking you tonight."

There was no question about who had brought her to orgasm on his tongue and fingers. Karl did not have to worry about that.

He nudged her drenched opening with the blunt tip of his cock. Nykee held her breath while he pushed forward. He rocked right into her, not allowing her time to adjust to his size. A cry tore from her at the slight pain that came but was gone in an instant. She had never felt this full before. Her walls screamed, adjusting to his size.

Karl pulled back slightly, leaving the tip inside her before thrusting home again.

Nykee's lungs burned, reminding her she needed to breathe. He repeated his motion again, lodging deep inside her. He brought her legs up and rested his hands on the backs of her thighs while he fucked her.

This wasn't a slow, gentle lovemaking.

No.

Not at all, and she wouldn't have it any other way.

His strokes were long and deep.

Nykee's moans grew louder. She reached over her head and gripped the sheets to hang on to something. Every muscle in her body grew tense. His cock pulsed inside her, her walls clamping around him.

"Nykee." Her name rolled out as a growl came from him.

She arched her back and thrust her hips forward to meet his every move.

He grew suddenly still. His eyes were clenched shut. Karl released her legs and propped his hands on the side of her head.

"What's wrong?" she whispered. She slid her hands along his slick chest. Both of their bodies were covered with a fine sheen of sweat. Her hands arrived at his jaw, and she cupped it. Willing him to open his eyes and look at her.

"Don't. Move," he rasped.

He opened his eyes, and there was a tortured look of ecstasy in them. She grinned internally. There was something about a man trying not to come that was so sexy.

"You mean like this?" She squeezed her core muscles around him.

He jerked his head in a nod.

"You're going to pay for that," he growled.

He withdrew from her and crushed his lips to hers. Their kiss was one of passion and pleasure. He released her and flipped her over before she even knew what was happening.

"Karl," she gasped, a giggle escaping her. She tried to push herself up on her hands and knees, but he pressed a hand on her back. "I misunderstood what you said."

"Sure." He pushed her facedown on the bed and lifted her hips. He used his knees to spread her legs apart.

A moan slipped from her at the sensation of his cock sliding through her drenched folds.

She cried out from his thick invasion. He sank deep inside her and held still for a moment before rocking back and thrusting hard.

The rhythm he set was brutal.

Nykee loved it.

She rocked her hips backwards to meet his demand. His length went deep, eliciting moans and cries from her.

"Karl," she chanted. Tears seeped from her eyes, blurring her vision. Not that she could see anything but the covers and mattress underneath her head.

He paused again, and this time he reached up and snagged her wrists in his hands and brought them behind her.

"Fuck, Nykee," he breathed.

That was all he had to say, and she knew she was in trouble. His hips moved as he took her hard and fast. All conscious thought left her. She could do nothing but focus on the pleasure roaring through her body.

The sounds of their lovemaking filled the air. Karl's hips slapped against her ass in a steady motion. It didn't take her long to reach her peak.

Nykee screamed into the mattress. Her body trembled and shook with the coursing sensations of her climax. A warmth filled her once Karl's roar echoed through the air. He released her arms and slipped one of his around her waist to hold her to him while he pressed himself to her and filled her with his release.

Karl withdrew from her and fell onto the bed next to her. He tugged her into his arms and held her.

Nykee flopped her arm across his waist and fell into a deep sleep.

10

Karl stared at the ceiling and didn't want to move.

He couldn't even if he tried.

Nykee held his arm hostage with her head. There wasn't an inch of her that didn't touch him at the moment. Her face was nestled in the crook of his neck while her curvy frame was planted along his side. Her warm breath fanned his skin with each breath she took.

To be honest, he was content where he was. Their night had been one of exploration, need, and desire. He was quite surprised her bed hadn't exploded into flames.

He gazed down at her soft brown skin and ran a hand along her arm that was wrapped across him possessively. His little sex kitten certainly had claws. His back was filled with scratches from Nykee's nails.

He didn't mind at all. It was proof that he had more than pleased her. His cock grew thick with the memories of their coupling.

"What time is it?" Nykee whispered. Her hand slid over his chest, her nails gently teasing his nipple.

"You got somewhere to go?" he murmured. He rested his hand on hers and moved his hand to her chin. He lifted it slightly to present her lips to him. He pressed a soft kiss to them, feeling them curve up into a smile.

"Nope. Just making sure you weren't trying to leave anytime soon."

"Ma'am, if you want me to leave, all you have to say is the word."

He rolled them over so she was lying on top of him. Her full breasts rested on his chest, and her knees automatically slid to his waist. She pushed up where he could see all of her. His breath caught in his throat at the magnificent sight before him. Her brown skin practically glowed in the low light. Her perky dark nipples were pebbled into little buds. He'd had multiple opportunities to taste them, and they were the sweetest he'd ever had.

He had finally got to explore her tattoos. She had many lining her forearms, and her right arm was almost completely covered. Her back even held a few, and he'd kissed every single one of them.

He slid his hands along her torso and landed at her hips. His cock, hard as steel, brushed her backside. He held back a groan. Nykee's stamina rivaled his own.

"Why would I want you to leave? I'm having too much fun with these." She pressed her fingers against his lips. Her eyes twinkled with mischief.

He captured her hand with his and licked her fingers. She giggled and tried to pull her arm back, but he held a firm grip on her while he ran his tongue along her fingers, reminding her of what he was capable of.

A gasp escaped her. She bit her lip while her gaze dropped to his mouth. She twisted around and took hold of his cock with her free hand.

"And I'm most definitely enjoying this right now." Her small hand stroked the length of him.

Karl's head dropped back onto his pillows. A moan was ripped from him at the feeling of her tugging on his hard length. His cock was enjoying itself as well. Her tight, warm sheath was heaven, and he was ready to slide back home into her.

"Is that right?" He tightened his hold on her hips.

He sat forward then leaned back against the headboard. He took her lips in a deep kiss. He pushed his tongue inside her mouth. Her tongue immediately met his. She wasn't shy when she kissed him. He slid his arm around to her back to hold her close to him. Her breasts brushed his chest and sent a growl escaping from him.

Nykee wrapped her arms around him. Her hips thrust forward again as she whimpered.

"Karl," Nykee gasped, breaking the kiss. She rested her forehead against his.

"What is it, baby?" he asked.

Her eyes closed, her breaths coming rapid. His heart raced at him feeling the heat of her core on him. His cock swelled even harder, needing her, but at the moment, he sensed she needed something from him.

"Don't hurt me," she whispered. Her fingers threaded their way into his hair. She opened her eyes and met his gaze. Fear was evident in them. "I'm assuming this is a one-time thing and I'm good with that."

"Nykee—"

"Please, let me finish." She placed a finger onto his mouth, stopping him.

He held her tighter in his arms. He already knew where she was going, but he would let her know that he wasn't just going to walk away from her.

Not after tonight.

She was a beautiful woman, inside and out, and he wanted her.

All of her.

He didn't care about her past or the mistakes she'd made.

He only knew he wanted to be a part of her present and her future.

Karl jerked his head in a nod.

"You are a good man, Karl. I can tell, and I'm not sure why you approached me, but I want to tell you that you've made me smile, laugh, and just feel like a woman, and I want to thank you. And if this is a one time and all I get, I'm okay with it. I'll still come to your family's cookout since Billie wants me there and I won't tell her about us—"

"I'm going to stop you while you're ahead of yourself." He couldn't allow her to keep going. Somehow, she had gotten all in her head and was thinking crazy.

How could he not want more than one night with her?

He offered her a smile and pressed a kiss to her fingers before removing them. He took them and rested her hand on his chest.

"I had never planned for this to be one night," he began. Karl had to concentrate on what he had to say. Her lovely body was proving to be a distraction.

She shifted slightly on his lap, her ass teasing his

cock. Her wide eyes locked on him, her lips parting slightly while she held on to his words.

"I knew from the moment we first met that I wanted to get to know you and that you were not a one-night stand kinda girl. I want to explore what this is between us. Everything about you intrigues me, and if you can't already tell, the chemistry between us isn't something that should be ignored."

Her shoulders relaxed. She leaned forward and softly kissed his lips.

"Are you sure? I come with a lot of baggage."

"I'm a strong man, Nykee," he teased, a smile playing on his lips. He squeezed her tight and kissed her chin, then trailed more kisses along her neck.

Her moan sent a wave of desire through him. He couldn't get enough of this woman. He cupped her full breasts. They filled his large hands perfectly.

"Karl," she breathed.

"I had planned to go slow with you." He grunted, lifting her.

He positioned the tip of his cock at her slick entrance. She rested her hands on his shoulders and slid down onto his length until he was fully sheathed inside her warm channel. Her muscles wrapped around him, holding him in place.

"Take my time until you were ready."

"Oh God, I'm ready," she uttered.

Her fingers threaded their way into his thick hair. Her grip on his strands didn't cause pain, but the sensation sent bolts of electricity through him. He nipped her neck and exhaled. Nykee rotated her hips, eliciting a groan from both of them.

He raised her again before impaling her on him. They fit perfectly together.

"Fuck." The air escaped him when she moved on her own.

He held on to her while she rode him. She looked like a Greek goddess riding along on her loyal stead.

He couldn't take his eyes off her.

Her head was thrown back as she took her pleasure. He allowed her to take what she needed from him. This was for her. Her hips bucked and gyrated and she increased her pace.

Unable to resist moving any longer, he thrust forward. He kept a firm hold on to her hips while he met her movements.

Nykee's head snapped forward. She gripped the sides of his face and brought him to her. Their lips merged into a hot, passionate kiss. Their tongues danced with each other, their bodies moved in tune together.

Moans, pants, and cries filled the air. The pleasure was mounting inside Karl. Nykee's fingers tightened in his hair.

He rolled his hips and pushed forward while pulling her down harder on him. Nykee's muscles tensed while her body trembled.

"Karl," she cried out.

"That's right, baby. Come for me," he rasped.

Her orgasm rocked through her body. Nykee's scream split through the silent room. The walls of her channel clamped down on him in a death grip. He rolled them over until she was on her back to allow him to take control.

His hips moved even faster, sending him farther into her. Nykee's legs wrapped around his waist as she met him thrust for thrust. He threw his bed back and roared through his release. He finally paused, the breath snatched from him as he poured himself into her.

❧

"You want me to do what?" Nykee stared at Foster. He couldn't have said what she thought he'd said. She sat on the floor of the house they shared and counted out the money stacks before her. She was one of the only people he trusted with his money. She was to count it and divide it up. He'd be taking it in the morning to go get 'cleaned.'

He stared at her while smoking a joint.

Foster Moss was a known drug dealer who had

captured her eye when she was still in high school. He'd driven the baddest cars, always flaunted his money, and for some reason, he'd approached Nykee. He was tall, dark, and handsome. His locks were shoulder-length, and his intense black eyes intrigued her.

But today, she didn't feel the way she had when she'd first got with him.

The status of 'girlfriend' for one of the largest known drug dealers wasn't all it was cracked up to be.

The thrill instantly went away the first time he'd put his hands on her. Or the times he'd openly cheated on her.

One of his goons, Freddie, sat on the couch with a smirk on his lips. She couldn't stand the guy and she hated the way he looked at her.

A shiver went through her.

She was sure the only reason Freddie hadn't done something to her was because she was Foster's woman. She heard plenty of talk that the man had raped quite a few women.

"You heard what I said. Don't be acting deaf now." Foster took another hit from the joint before passing it to Freddie. He leaned forward and rested his elbows on his knees. Those dark eyes of his stared at her. "You're going to run this next deal. I can't send any of my men in there because of bad blood. They want the product, and I'm going to give it to them to smooth out the animosity."

"So all I have to do is drop off a package." She swallowed hard. Something about this just didn't add up with

her. Foster had plenty of runners he could use to drop off packages. Why her?

Freddie snickered when he took his hit of the small joint. He knew something but wasn't going to say. He was loyal to Foster and didn't really care about Nykee. He kept his atten-tion on the basketball game on the television.

Nykee didn't like the sound of this.

"Me sending my woman in with the package will be considered a peace offering." Foster leaned back in his chair.

"Yo, Foster. We're done." A young woman appeared in the doorway. She wore the standard clothing allotted for the girls who prepped the drugs for him in the basement. One of his guards stood behind her with his arms folded. "And we're hungry, too."

Nykee stared down at the table in front of her. This young girl was one who Foster had fucked. He'd claimed to Nykee that it of course didn't mean anything and it was his way of ensuring her loyalty to him.

"Who the fuck do you think you're talking to?" Foster snarled.

Foster stood and stalked over to the girl. Her scream echoed after the sound of his hand struck her.

Nykee hadn't even taken the time to learn her name. She didn't know any of the women's names who worked for him in the basement. None of them ever stayed around, and Nykee had always been afraid to ask what happened to them.

"Sorry, boss. She said she had an important question to ask you," the guard said.

"Take her ass back downstairs. Tell Mano to bring in the second load for them." Foster went back over to his chair and sat. He took the joint from Freddie and inhaled sharply.

"Yes, sir." The guard snagged the sniffling woman by her arm and practically dragged her back down the hallway.

"Bitches have some nerve," Freddie muttered. He crossed his legs and focused back on the game.

"Nykee," Foster snapped.

She glanced up and caught sight of him waving her over to him. She stood immediately and went to him, not wanting him to turn his wrath on her. His gaze roamed over her and darkened. She was dressed in cotton shorts and a t-shirt, and he was totally undressing her with his eyes. She knew the look, and it wouldn't be much longer before she'd be flat on her back.

He grinned and snagged her arm to pull her onto his lap. That smile of his had been what lured her to him. He had appeared nice and handsome when they had met. He'd given her everything and anything she'd asked for.

She settled on his lap astride him. He adjusted her knees so they rested either side of his waist. He reached up and brushed her hair from her face and took in her features.

"You love me, right?" he asked. He handed off the joint to Freddie without taking his gaze from her.

She jerked her head in a nod.

Was she still in love with him?

No.

But she dared not reveal the truth.

Honestly, she was stuck with him. How could she return home to her family? She wasn't the good girl like her sister, Bashara, and she certainly wasn't like her brother, Jimar. She was the failure of the family. The one child who her parents couldn't brag about. She tried to stay away from them, embarrassed at the life she led. As she'd grew older, she'd realized what she had truly gotten into.

And she wanted out of this lifestyle.

But that was going to prove to be hard to do since Foster was possessive.

There was no leaving him until he was done with you.

"Of course I do, baby." The words felt stale spilling from her lips. She smiled and rested a hand on his that cupped her cheek. As long as she played the sweet, loving girlfriend, she would be okay. He loved when she praised him and made it appear she wouldn't make it without him.

"Good. You do this favor for me, and I'll make sure you are rewarded."

He placed a kiss to her lips. His hand slid down to her throat. Her heart skipped a beat before racing. The smile disappeared from his lips while a scowl formed on his face. He applied slight pressure to her neck.

"You do whatever he wants you to do. If he wants your pussy, you give it to him."

. . .

Nykee jerked forward with a cry. She blinked a few times and took in her surroundings. She was in her home in Shady Springs and safe.

"What's wrong?" Strong arms wrapped around her.

Karl.

Nykee relaxed and leaned into his embrace. He guided them back onto the bed and pulled her back to him. He adjusted the covers and kissed her bare shoulder.

"It's nothing. Just a bad dream," she whispered. Nykee inhaled sharply and took in the scent of the man holding her.

She was safe.

She chanted this repeatedly in her head.

"Are you sure?" He ran his hand along her arms.

Her body trembled from the fear that had encapsulated her while she was deep in her nightmare. She didn't want to relive that part of her life again.

Foster was gone.

Nykee didn't have to worry about him. She may have only had to do a few years in prison, but he got the max sentence for his crimes and sentenced to twenty-five years. She hadn't heard from him in years and would never again. She'd cut all ties from her former life.

It was behind her, and she would never go back to it.

She had something good going for her and now she had a man who wanted her, just for her. She glanced over her shoulder and took in Karl's concerned look.

"I'm sure." She snuggled into his embrace and was met with his hardness pressing against her bottom. A grin snuck its way onto her lips. How could he be hard again?

"Well, I sure didn't like the sounds you were making." Karl dropped another kiss to her shoulder. His hand snuck around and cupped her pussy. He pushed a finger into her folds and groaned.

"I'll be okay. Maybe you can chase away those bad dreams."

She whimpered. His finger dipped into her wet heat. The man definitely did something to her body. She was constantly wet and horny for him. He toyed with her clit, eliciting a whimper from her.

"You want me to make you feel good, is that it?"

His hot breath skated along her ear, sending shivers down her spine. He lifted her leg and, moments later, his cock sank deep inside her from behind.

"Yes," she hissed. The remnants of her dream were slowly fading away. She focused on the sensation of Karl filling her. It felt so good, and she could no longer think of anything else.

"I got you."

Nykee cried out when he pounded into her. Pleasure flooded Nykee, wiping away all thoughts from her. The only thing left was Karl.

He lifted her leg higher and went deeper.

He apparently knew just what she needed.

❧ 11 ❧

"Where do you want this?" Karl asked. He carried the two foldable tables out of the store shed on his parents' property.

"Put that over there with the rest of them. We're going to load up your father's truck. The park has some tables, but it doesn't have enough." Billie pointed to the wide tree near the detached three-car garage.

"Who all are you inviting to the cookout?" Kaden groaned. He followed behind Karl with metal chairs.

The sun was shining, and it was a beautiful day. The Tanis gathering was one of the biggest in the county. Billie knew how to throw a party. Each year more people showed up.

"You know she invites the entire state," Karl

teased. He tossed a wink to his mother who waved her hands at him.

"It's so much fun, and what better way to get caught up with family and friends."

"Maybe try social media?" Kaden snorted.

They sat the table and chairs where she had instructed.

"That's no fun. I tried getting on that Handbook or Stampgram, whatever it's called, but I just don't understand it. Why do I need to see pictures of people's food and they not just invite me over to enjoy it with them?" She shrugged.

Karl chuckled at his mother. She wasn't as old as she made herself to be, but online things weren't for her. She was such a social butterfly that being in the presence of people was more her thing.

Their father, on the other hand, was an introvert who adored their mother so much he put up with her parties.

Daisy barked and stood on the top stair of the back porch.

"What's her problem?" he asked, eyeing the dog.

Billie turned and picked her up and carried her down the stairs.

"Oh, nothing. She just needs to do her business." Billie placed her down on the ground. The dog scampered off and went over by the corner of the house and squatted.

"Seriously? You had to carry her down the stairs?" Kaden shook his head and barked a laugh. "I remember that time I was scared to take the stairs and you made me slide down them."

Karl wrapped an arm around his younger brother's shoulders as they walked over to their mother.

"Yeah, and if I recall, you pissed yourself, too."

"You son of a—" Kaden pushed him off and playfully threw a jab his way.

Karl blocked it and sent one of his own.

Karl loved spending time with his family. Growing up, he and his brother spent plenty of times sparring with each other. Kaden had joined the local boxing club and had boxed on the amateur level.

"Now, now. Don't let me have to teach you a lesson." Karl snickered.

They circled each other, sizing each other up.

"In your dreams, old man," Kaden scoffed.

Karl was only five years older than his brother. Kaden and Nykee were the same age.

Nykee's face came to mind. It had been almost a week since their first date. Each day after work, he'd gone to see her or she'd come to his home. They were inseparable, and he was loving how much time he'd got to spend with her and how close they were growing.

She was just as special as he knew she would be.

The only thing that bothered him was these nightmares she'd experienced.

She didn't talk about it much, but he hoped she'd soon open up to him. He wanted to help her. They'd spent the night a few times since then, and she'd had one each time.

Every time, she woke up and turned to him.

He knew what she needed.

Whatever she dreamed about, she wanted to forget it.

And he rose to the challenge every single time.

Pain exploded on his chin. He blinked, his head jerking back from Kaden landing a blow.

"Caught you daydreaming, huh?"

Karl stumbled back and laughed. His brother grinned at him. Karl had never let his little brother best him before. How would that ever look that his little brother could take him?

"Y'all stop before someone gets hurt!" Billie hollered from the porch. "I'm not taking anyone to the hospital."

She walked down the stairs and headed in their direction.

"I guess there's a first time for everything." Karl

wiped his lip and glanced down at his hand. A small smudge of redness greeted him.

Dammit, Kaden had busted his lip.

Daisy ran around his feet, barking and jumping up on him.

"Whatever, bro. I've whipped your ass before," Kaden teased.

"You attacking while I'm asleep does not count," Karl scoffed. Daisy was intent on getting his attention. He leaned down and scooped her up. "What is it, dog?"

She yapped and tried to lick him on his face. He held her back and shook his head.

"No kisses," he muttered.

"She's just trying to show you her appreciation for taking her to her appointment." Billie laughed. She took Daisy from him and cradled her in her arms. "Ain't that right, girl?"

"It was no problem." He instantly thought of what he'd gained for taking the dog for her spa day. Just in that short time, he'd met a woman who he wouldn't mind becoming committed to. Nykee was special, and he wasn't going to waste any time ensuring that woman was his.

"Nykee is coming, right?" she asked, turning her bright-blue eyes to him.

Karl smirked. He reached up and rummaged a

hand through his hair. He might as well get this over with instead of surprising his mother at the gathering.

"Yeah, I'm bringing her," he said.

"Oh, did she need a ride?"

"Who's Nykee?" Kaden asked.

"Daisy's groomer. She's a wonderful girl, and her and I just hit it off. She's a shy girl, but I wanted her to come so she can get out and meet people. She's had a hard time in life and she's doing well for herself." Billie's eyes lit up as she spoke highly of Nykee. She turned back to Karl. "Do I need to send someone to get her?"

"No, Mom. She's coming with me," he emphasized, trying to keep the wide grin from spreading across his face.

Billie paused. Her eyes grew wide as understanding hit her.

"Really? As in a date?" she squealed. His mother hopped up and down, and Daisy barked.

"Yeah, we've already gone out together," he continued. He would leave out certain details that his mother didn't need to know.

"Wait? Mom is playing matchmaker now?" Kaden wrapped an arm around Billie's shoulders.

They walked toward the front of the house. Their father should be back with his pickup soon so they could load the tables and chairs to take over to the park.

"I honestly didn't think anything of it," Billie gushed. Her eyes twinkled.

Karl knew she was lying.

But he was okay with it.

She'd done good.

"I had to take Momma to her appointments and I didn't have a way for Daisy to get to her appointment because you know your father wasn't going to do it." She laughed.

"You didn't call me." Kaden raised an eyebrow.

"She called her favorite son," Karl interjected.

Kaden's eyes whipped toward him. It had always been a thing between them on who was the favorite son. Plenty of scuffles in the past because of it.

It was all in good nature. The Tanis family was competitive, and naturally, both of them always wanted to be the favorite son.

"You son of a bitch." Kaden ran at him.

Karl grinned and took off running toward the front yard with Kaden hot on his tail.

"There are no favorites!" Billie yelled out, but they ignored her as they always did.

Kaden caught up and crashed into him. His arms wrapped around Karl, and he lifted him off the ground.

"I should slam your ass," Kaden joked. He set him down just as their father's truck drove down the long driveway.

Karl grabbed his brother around the neck and walked toward their father's parked truck. He couldn't wait for Kaden and Nykee to meet. He was sure they would get along just fine.

"What are you boys tussling about now?" Briggs asked, stepping from his truck. He was a large, stocky man. Both Karl and Kaden resembled him. They had his dark hair, same colored eyes and build. Only the old man had gained weight around the middle and blamed it on their mother's cooking ever since he'd retired.

"They are just being boys, even though they are in their thirties." Billie rolled her eyes.

Briggs dropped a kiss on her lips before turning toward them. Their parents had been together almost forty years and were still very much in love.

Karl envied their relationship. He hoped to have half of what they had. Images of Nykee floated through his mind. She was someone who he was finding he loved being around. Her laugh was infectious, her beauty mesmerizing, and the sounds she made coming on his cock had him officially addicted to her.

"What can I say besides I'm young at heart," Karl

joked. He pushed Kaden away from him, landing a soft jab to the shoulder.

They arrived at their parents, and each of them gave Briggs a manly hug, slapping each other on the back.

"Plus, Kaden is jealous of me, as always."

"Don't listen to him, Pop." Kaden folded his arms in front of him. He scrubbed a hand along his jawline. "I have plenty of women lining up trying to get a piece of me."

"Of course. A woman. I should have known." Briggs chuckled. His hazel-eyed gaze landed on Karl. "Who is she?"

"Nykee, Daisy's groomer," Billie gushed. Her grin widened. Daisy wiggled down from her arms and dropped to the ground. She scampered off, sniffing the grass. "She's a wonderful girl, Briggs. I'm so happy they hit it off."

"This the girl you was talking about that you wanted to hook Karl up with?" Briggs said. He removed his wide-brimmed hat and threaded his fingers through his hair.

"Briggs!" Billie's wide eyes flicked to Karl before going back to her husband. "You weren't supposed to say anything."

They shared a laugh, watching her cheeks deepen.

Karl stepped forward and wrapped her up in a strong hug.

"You did good, Ma. I really like her." He pressed a kiss to her temple.

"Good. Now I'll work on your brother next," she whispered.

Her eyes twinkled, and Karl glanced over at his brother who was speaking with their father.

Kaden didn't stand a chance.

KARL ASSESSED HIS SHOPPING CART AND TRIED TO see if he was missing anything. Tonight he was cooking dinner for Nykee. He wanted it to be perfect. He'd picked out great steaks that had beautiful marbling on them and a few big fat potatoes that he was going to bake for her. It was one of his favorite meals. He was a big man and needed hearty meals to sustain him with the calories burned when working on a ranch.

"Ah, almost forgot," he murmured.

Wine.

Couldn't have a good meal like this and not have something to wash it down with. He pushed his grocery cart down the aisle and turned the corner.

He jerked to a stop, almost running into Deputy Griffen.

"Excuse me," Karl said instantly. He pulled his cart back, to avoid hitting the deputy.

Griffen was dressed in his uniform and didn't look as if he were shopping in the store. Shady Springs was a small town, and the deputy was probably stopping in as part of his route.

"Hey, Karl. How are you?" Griffen nodded.

"I'm good. How about yourself?" Karl didn't really care, but it was polite to ask. He eyed the deputy warily. He hadn't forgotten their last encounter. It had left a bad taste in his mouth.

It was easy to see that the deputy wanted to find a reason to arrest Nykee. Why else would he harass her when she was doing no wrong and then tried to warn him off her?

"Doing well. I hope you took into consideration what I said the other night." Griffen folded his arms in front of him.

Karl met his unwavering gaze.

"Wasn't looking for any advice." Karl shook his head slowly. He held back the sneer that wanted to form on his lips.

"That's too bad. Don't say I didn't warn you about that girl. She's nothing—"

"You don't know her or the woman she's become." Karl stood to his full height.

"I know Nykee, and people like her don't change."

"People like her? What are you trying to say?" Karl clenched his fist together. He hated bullies, and at the moment, Griffen was one, and he wasn't going to stand by and let him attack Nykee.

"I'm saying people who led a life of crime just don't change overnight. She may have you fooled, but not me."

"Well, it's a good thing she doesn't care what you think." Karl snatched his cart and pushed it away from the deputy. Today was not a day he wanted to get arrested for assaulting a man of the law.

He quickly went and found a good bottle of wine that should pair well with what he had planned. After checking out, he walked to his truck. His gaze landed on the police cruiser parked in front of the grocery store. Anger riled up in him, but he pushed it down.

Nykee had done no wrong, and it wasn't fair the police were trying to sniff around her to find something to pin on her. He wasn't sure what she had been involved in the past, but he knew she was a good woman and a standup citizen now.

Karl threw his bags in his truck and got in. The ride home was done in silence. He had to try to force himself to calm down. He didn't want Nykee to know what had happened in the grocery store. She'd already tried to shut him down at the park when Griffen had made reference to her past.

Those nightmares of hers were surely connected to something that haunted her.

He couldn't chance she'd find out. Deep down, he wanted to know all of her secrets, the good and the bad.

But he'd have to let her come to him.

Once she was ready, he'd sit back and listen to her with an open heart.

12

Nykee pulled into her driveway and killed her engine. Karl had invited her over to dinner after work, and she wanted to stop home and shower before heading over there.

No way was she going to show up smelling like dogs and sweat.

Nykee's excitement filled her. Tonight, she probably wasn't going to be leaving his place. Karl had grumbled the last time she'd left late to return home.

"Let me get my spend-a-night bag ready." She grinned and hopped out of the car. She slammed the door shut and made her way to her porch. A package sitting by her front door was a surprise. "I didn't order anything."

At least not lately.

She did have an obsession with a certain online store that always got her items delivered quickly.

Jogging up her stairs, she picked up the box and confirmed it wasn't hers. It was addressed to Mrs. Chambers who lived across the street.

"Just great." Nykee sighed. She didn't have much time, and she dare not keep the box for now. She might as well run it over to her. She hefted her purse up on her shoulder and walked toward the street. She paused as a few cars went by in passing.

Her neighborhood was small, and she only was familiar with a few of the people who resided near her. Nykee mostly kept to herself. Word always get around Shady Springs fast, and she didn't want to deal with anyone who may have issues with her.

Nykee had learned that most people didn't have an open mind.

She just didn't have time for those types of people.

The homes that faced Nykee's were positioned farther away from the road than the houses on Nykee's side of the street. She marched over to Mrs. Chambers' home and down her long driveway. It was a beautiful day, and the sun was shining bright.

Nykee was in a good mood, and this little hiccup wasn't going to slow her down. She'd run home, shower, pick out a cute outfit, and throw a bag together. She wouldn't even tell Karl. She'd just leave it on her back seat.

Nykee arrived at the front of the house, but the sign on the door asking for packages to be left in the back caught her eye. She continued on towards the back of the house.

Barking cut through the air. She took in a few dogs in a caged-in area. She grinned at them and waved. She was familiar with Dusky, a chocolate Lab who always seemed to get out of the enclosure and roam around her yard.

Placing the package on the edge of the small porch, she gave another wave at the dogs who were frantically barking and pacing back and forth. She grinned and made her way back to the street. She paused, waiting for a chance to cross. The road she lived in tended to be busy after work as everyone raced to get home. She glanced over and saw one of the Mrs. Chambers' neighbors sitting in her rocking chair on her porch.

"Howdy," Nykee called out.

The old woman didn't return her greeting but kept rocking. She raised her coffee mug to her lips, took a drink, and turned her head in the opposite direction.

Nykee faced the street. "Okay."

The road cleared, and Nykee jogged across it. She

was not going to allow a little old lady to ruin her day.

Nykee went into her home and shut the door. She tossed her keys in the bowl by the door and her purse on the couch. She flew into her bedroom and kicked her shoes off. She tore her clothes off and threw them into her hamper.

Grabbing her towel, she went into the bathroom and turned the water on to allow it to get warm.

She hummed while wrapping her hair and tying her silk scarf around it. Nykee paused and stared at herself in the mirror.

She couldn't remember a time she'd been this happy.

Looking at herself, she turned to the side and took in her little pouch of a stomach. She held it in and knew she could stand to lose some weight, but it didn't seem to bother Karl. He always made sure to love on every part of her.

How did she get so lucky to meet someone like him?

Tonight, they'd stay in for a date, and tomorrow was his family's cookout.

It was crazy how time had flown by. It all just seemed to be too good to be true. She kept waiting for something to ruin what they had.

Karl was too good for her, but the man upstairs

must have wanted to reward her for something she'd done. She didn't know what, but she wasn't going to let this thing with Karl go. She deserved happiness.

What the Fluff was doing well.

She had her health and family.

Now she had Karl.

A grin spread across her face.

Yes, this was the life she'd wanted. To be successful, have the love of her family and a trustworthy man.

She had thought she might end up alone for the rest of her life. Not that there would have been anything wrong with that, but she secretly always wanted what her parents had.

One day, she hoped children would be in the works. The thought of her belly swelling with Karl's child took her breath away.

Would he want that type of future with her? He wanted her now, but could what they had now blossom into something more?

Something more long-term?

"You're putting the cart before the horse." Nykee sighed. She walked over to the shower and got in. The warm water sliding along her tired muscles felt amazing. She grabbed her loofah and squirted some of her shower gel onto it. She washed all of the grime from her body until she was squeaky clean.

Once done, she exited the shower and went back into her room. She had to find the right outfit that didn't give too much away. It was warm outside, so she settled on a sleeveless maxi dress that highlighted her curves. She had bought it on a whim, and it looked as if she finally had a reason to wear it.

She laid it on her bed and went over to her dresser and snagged a sexy set of undergarments to wear and put them on. Soon she was dressed, smelling fresh, and had her hair done. She worked on her overnight bag next.

What did one pack when they were spending the night over at a man's home?

She stood beside her bed and stared down at the nighty she had in her hand. Would she really need it? The couple of times she'd slept with Karl, there hadn't been any clothes involved.

She put it in the bag. It probably wouldn't make its way out because she would need more than just her clothes for tomorrow and her toothbrush. It had been a long while since she had to worry about pleasing a man.

She didn't know what to wear for the cookout, so she grabbed two outfits. A summer dress and a t-shirt and shorts. She'd decide tomorrow.

Once she was finished, she zipped up the bag and

padded into the living room. She dropped it by the door before doing a sweep through her home to make sure her back door was locked. She left the lamp on in the living room and snagged her purse and keys.

Lately, she was finding she had a permanent grin on her lips when thinking of Karl. Korah and Blake had teased her unmercifully at work. They had caught Nora up on her new romance.

She grabbed her purse and headed outside. She locked her door and spun around. Her gaze landed on the old lady who was still seated on her porch across the street. With a shrug, Nykee got into her car and wouldn't give the lady another inch of space in her mind.

Her phone signaled a text. She pulled it out of her purse and saw a message from Karl.

I can't wait to see you.

Her smile widened. Her heart rate spiked. The man just had her feeling all good inside. She found herself thinking of him nonstop at work.

Good things come to those who wait.

She sent off her reply then started her car.

Her notification sounded almost immediately.

Don't make me wait too long.

If someone would have told Nykee three years ago that there was a man out there who would bring a smile to her lips and have her giggling like a young schoolgirl, she would have called them crazy.

But here she was.

She tossed her phone in her purse and put her car in reverse. She backed out of her drive and guided her car onto the road. She couldn't get the smile off her face.

Her phone rang, and her sister's name appeared on the dash screen.

"Hey, sis," she answered.

"Hey, what you doing?" Shara asked.

"Um, on my way to Karl's house," she replied. Nykee grimaced, remembering she had never called her sister back to update her.

"Oh, so we're seeing him again..." Her sister's voice turned teasing.

"Yes, and I'm sorry that I didn't call you back."

"I've been waiting by the phone, hoping you'd call me."

Nykee rolled her eyes.

"You are the one leading an exciting life. I've been living through you vicariously." Nykee snorted.

Shara and Rick were the couple everyone envied. Her husband was a sports newscaster who reported on the local Chicago sports teams. He had played football in the NFL for two years before getting injured. They'd decided to stay in Chicago for his job and to raise their children.

"Well, now it's your turn to have the exciting life. I put on sexy lingerie, and Rick barely sees it anymore." Shara laughed. She deepened her voice to imitate her husband, "Why you got that on for?"

"Because maybe he just wants the goods. Can't blame a man for being straightforward." Nykee laughed.

Her sister and husband were madly in love with each other. Rick practically worshipped the ground Shara walked on.

"Well, when I spend money on pretty things, I want him to appreciate them, too," Shara huffed.

"Maybe he likes them better on the floor." Nykee snickered.

"Have you been talking to Rick, because that's what he said."

They fell into a fit of giggles. Nykee couldn't wait to see her sister whenever she decided to come to town.

"Well, Miss Thing," Shara said, "since you are going over your new boy toy's house, I want a picture."

"What?"

"Not a naked nasty picture, but one where I can

see who has my sister buying lingerie and going out on dates, leaving her too busy for me."

"You are crazy." Nykee shook her head. She bit her lip, trying to think of a sly way to get a picture of Karl without him thinking she was weird.

"I'm serious. I won't be in town for a couple more weeks, and it's going to kill me to not know what this guy looks like." Her sister's voice turned whiny.

"Okay." Nykee rolled her eyes again. She slowed down at the intersection that led to Karl's house. A couple of cars drove past her before she turned. She gripped the steering wheel tight. She could do this. She wasn't much of a selfie taker when it came to her smart phone, but for her sister who didn't ask much of her, she would do it.

"Yay!" Nykee could hear Shara practically dancing through the phone.

"Hey, I got to go. I will talk to you later and I promise I will send a picture tonight."

They quickly said their goodbyes and ended the call.

Nykee drove the rest of the trip silent, barely hearing the music playing on the radio. She soon found herself pulling into his driveway and parked alongside his pickup.

She shut off the engine and glanced in the rearview mirror at her bag sitting on the seat. She would leave it in here for now. She didn't want to invite herself to stay the night. If the offer was made, then she'd be ready.

Blowing out a deep breath, she exited her vehicle and walked up to the house. The door opened before she'd even got to the stairs.

"It's about time," Karl drawled, standing in the doorway.

Her tongue stuck to the roof of her mouth. He was dressed in a navy-blue and white plaid flannel shirt where the top two buttons were undone. The sleeves were folded up his forearms, his jeans hugged his muscles, and he was barefoot.

"Hey." She smiled.

She walked up the stairs and crossed over the threshold. He closed the door and slid an arm around her waist, bringing her flush to him. His head swooped down, and he captured her lips in a blazing-hot kiss. Nykee locked her knees to prevent them from giving way.

Karl drew back slightly with that damn sexy grin of his plastered on his face. His hazel eyes twinkled with mischief.

"I missed you," he murmured. He dropped another kiss on her lips then took her hand in his. "Come on. Let me feed you."

13

K arl had to keep his distance from Nykee. From the moment she'd arrived, he'd wanted to toss her over his shoulder and whisk her off to his bedroom and lock them away for hours.

He would save that for later. Right now, he needed to feed her. He was sure she was hungry since she had worked all day. The wine was chilling, and he had saved the steaks for last so he could throw them on the grill. He wanted to make tonight special.

"This smells so wonderful," she exclaimed. Her hand tightened on his as he led them into the kitchen.

"I'm glad you think so." He took her over to the island. He didn't want to let her go, but he needed both hands to take the wine and glasses out.

"Didn't you go to work?" She laughed. She leaned against the counter and folded her arms in front of her.

"I did, and this didn't take me long to put together." He pulled the wine and glasses out and set them down beside her. He took care opening the wine and dropped the cork on to the counter.

She watched him with her pretty brown eyes while he poured them hefty glasses.

"Are you trying to get me tipsy, Mr. Tanis?" Her eyebrow jerked up high.

"Not at all." He smirked and moved close to her. He raised his glass to hers and waited for her to tap hers to his.

"What are you toasting?" Nykee asked.

"New beginnings," he murmured.

Her eyes darkened, and she bit her lip. She slowly raised her glass to his, and the sound of them clinking echoed through the air.

"New beginnings," she repeated. They took a sip of the wine, not breaking eye contact. "And what new beginnings are we talking about?"

"Oh, seeing how we are in a relationship and it's new, I thought it would be best that we recognize it."

"We're in a relationship?"

"What?" He feigned as if hurt. His hand flew up to his chest and rested over his heart.

Her giggle erupted, and his dick twitched at the sound of it. Her laughter was something he always wanted to hear. She fell back against the island, laughing. It was then he realized she just didn't see how beautiful she was and that he wanted more than just a casual fuck. His smile slipped from his lips. He had to make sure she knew this honestly wasn't a game.

"Are you serious? Do you not realize how much I want you? How much I want you to be mine?"

Her smile slowly faded. Her gaze dropped down to the buttons of his shirt. He reached out and tipped her chin up so he could meet her gaze.

"I guess it's hard for me to believe anyone truly wants me," she whispered.

Karl pushed down the anger that threatened to rise. He didn't know what the men in her past had done, but they had certainly done a number on her self-confidence.

"You are a beautiful woman, smart, sexy, and from now on, mine." He lowered his head to hers and took her lips in a possessive kiss. He didn't care how long they had known each other. He knew he wanted to learn everything about her, spend time with her, slip into her heated core, and feel her shatter in his arms.

This woman deserved love, and he wanted to be the one to give it to her.

He pulled back and watched her open her eyes one at a time.

"Now, as I was saying, to new beginnings." He held up his glass again.

She didn't hesitate to press hers to his.

"New beginnings." This time her voice was stronger, and her smile was wide and genuine.

"Now, let's go out onto the patio where I have the grill waiting to receive our steaks." He slipped an arm around her waist and guided her out the sliding glass doors.

He and his brother had built an outdoor kitchen on his patio. When he'd purchased the home, he'd fallen in love with the backyard that overlooked rolling hills. He had designed the patio to be an outdoor living area where he could have guests over to entertain.

They'd even installed a hot tub for those nights when he'd worked his body sore. He'd spent plenty of time in the tub to relax and release the tension from his muscles.

"What is this?" Nykee gasped. She paused next to him, her gaze on the table.

He had never gone this far out for a woman before. He'd decorated the table with a floral arrangement he'd picked up on the way home. The table was set with the nice dinnerware his mother had insisted he needed. There was a string of soft lights twinkling around the ceiling.

Soft music played through the hidden speakers, while there were candles on the table to enhance the ambiance.

He'd wanted to impress Nykee and show her how special she was to him. It was simple, but he wanted to show he was making an effort.

"You like it?" he asked. He stepped away from her to get a good look at her face.

She jerked her head in a nod and took a hefty sip of her wine.

'It's beautiful," she whispered.

"Come, let me feed you." He escorted her over to the table and assisted her to her seat. He finished off his wine in one gulp and set the empty glass down on the table near his spot. "You relax right there, while I finish up dinner."

"I'm not going anywhere."

NYKEE WOULD HAVE TO ADMIT WHEN KARL FIRST said he was going to cook for them, she'd thought a simple dinner.

But no.

Karl had taken the time to ensure their dinner date in his home was special. She was floored with all of the thought and preparation he had put into planning tonight. His backyard held a beautiful backdrop for them.

The steaks had been cooked how she preferred them, and the potatoes were to die for. How did she get so lucky to find a hardworking man with a good head on his shoulders who came from a wonderful family and could cook?

She kept expecting something to pop up to ruin everything between her and Karl, but so far—nothing.

"The yard is beautiful," she murmured.

They were sitting on the small sofa. Nykee's belly was full of good food and wine. Karl's arm was propped along the back of the furniture, allowing her to snuggle into his side.

This was the perfect date.

She didn't need fancy things she saw people post on social media.

This was what pleased her.

"Wait until the wintertime when the snow falls. It reminds me of a Hallmark Christmas card."

"I love the wintertime and snow. I am a very good snowman builder," she bragged.

It was something her and her siblings had done each winter. Their yard would be decorated with a snow family. She hadn't thought about that in years. She'd have to text her siblings about it. They would have to do it again this year for Christmas when they gathered at their parents' house for the holiday.

"Well, when it snows, I expect to have a fancy snowman built just for me. I'll even get his clothing he'll need."

They shared a chuckle with Nykee promising to build him his own snowman.

"So about tomorrow," Nykee began. She was a little nervous to be going to his family cookout. The only other person she would know was Billie.

"You're not trying to back out of going, are you?" he asked.

"No, not at all. I'm just wondering, how many people will be there?" She bit her lip. Large crowds weren't her thing. The only reason she had agreed to go was because of Billie. She had originally planned to arrive, show her face, stay maybe about an hour, and then make up an excuse on why she had to leave early. That plan wouldn't work now that she was going with Karl.

"My mother has the habit of inviting anyone who shares our last name, her side of the family, and any person who resides in our county."

That Nykee could believe. Billie was such a social butterfly. She'd make friends with the entire state if she could.

Karl glanced at her and squeezed her shoulder. "You won't have to worry. You'll be with me, and I'll introduce you around."

"Okay, just don't leave me." A nervous chuckle escaped her.

"Don't worry. You'll be fine. Everyone is going to love you." He dropped a kiss on her forehead. "My family is about as crazy as me."

Nykee grew quiet and rested her head on his shoulder. This was the most relaxed and comfortable she'd felt in years. She would have to trust Karl about tomorrow. It was hard for her to trust a person when they first met. She could thank Foster for that.

But Karl wasn't Foster.

He wouldn't do any of the things her former boyfriend had made her do.

Since you are going over your new boy toy's house, I want a picture.

Her sister's words came to mind. Her phone was sitting on the cushion next to her. She eyed it. Did she have the courage to take a selfie with him? Would he care? She glanced over at him and caught him smiling at her.

"What's going on in that beautiful brain of yours?" he asked.

It was now or never.

She snatched up her phone and hit the photo app. She didn't take that many selfies, but she had to do this one. Shara would never leave her be if she didn't.

"I want you to take a picture with me," she said. She leaned into him and turned the phone to capture the two of them. Her heart raced as he tugged her even closer. His warm breath caressed the lobe of her ear. A shiver rippled through her. She bit her lip, feeling the familiar sensations of her body responding to Karl. Her core clenched with need as his hand came to rest on her belly just below her breast.

They came into view on the screen, and she had to admit they looked good together. She snapped the picture. A laughed escaped her when he nuzzled his face into the crook of her neck. Her body jerked from the onslaught of his fingers digging into her side. She was very ticklish and had forgotten how much so.

A scream erupted from her as she tried to get away.

"Where do you think you're going?" He laughed.

He pulled her back to him and swiped her phone from her hand. "Let me show you how to take a proper picture."

He brought her up onto his lap and held the phone away with his long arms. She wrapped her arms around his neck and leaned her head against his. He snapped a few pictures of them before handing her back the phone.

"How are you so proficient with selfies?" she asked.

"It pays to have younger cousins who are in their late teens and early twenties." He grimaced.

She barked a laugh, trying to imagine him taking photos with his cousins.

He rested his chin on her shoulder while she looked through the pictures. She finally chose one and sent it off to her sister.

"And who are you showing me off to?" he asked, his tone light and teasing.

Her face warmed in embarrassment.

"My sister wanted to see what you looked like," she admitted.

"Oh, so talking about me with your sister, huh?" His eyebrow rose up high. That crooked grin of his expanded wider.

"She was curious—"

"I'm just messing with you." He kissed her lips and wrapped his arms around her tighter. "I don't mind at all. I think it's cute you're sending our pic to your sister."

"We are close," she whispered. Her phone vibrated, signaling a response. She glanced down at her phone, a gasp escaping her.

Holy hell, sis. Lock that down!

"What'd she say?" His hand cradled hers that held her phone and tilted it so he could read her sister's text.

Nykee groaned and closed her eyes. His deep chuckle rumbled in her ears.

"Go ahead and reply. I want to see what you say." His eyes were issuing a challenge.

She stared into his hazel orbs, and her core quivered.

This man had a way about him that drew her to him.

She bit her lip and turned her focus back to her phone.

Don't worry. I have.

His body shook with laughter as he peeked over her shoulder and took in what she sent to her sister. A sheepish grin spread across her face. This was the new Nykee, and she was liking this.

"What else have you got planned for us?" she

asked, trying to change the subject. She dropped her phone back down on the cushion and shifted around on his lap so she could see him.

So far, he had planned a wonderful dinner for them. Their conversation never stalled. They spoke of their childhood. She'd learned so much about Karl and his family. He and his brother were extremely close. She had been hesitant to share certain parts of her life with Karl. He hadn't pushed her, and she appreciated it.

She was truthfully embarrassed of her previous life and the decisions she had made. He'd come from a good family just as she did, but she'd followed the wrong path. Anything she shared was just about her immediate family and her younger years.

She didn't have fun stories from college to share like he had. Her stories would include nights spent in clubs, drugs, and violence she'd witnessed or been a victim of.

That wasn't something she wanted to share with anyone. Nykee was trying to leave the past where it belonged.

Behind her.

"Well, that would depend." Karl shrugged.

"On what?"

"On how long you're staying." His gaze landed on her.

She swallowed back her grin and dropped her gaze down to his shirt. She reached up and played with his shirt.

"What if I told you that I have a bag in my car so I can spend the night?" she drawled. She looked up and caught the smirk on his lips.

"I knew it." He grinned. He swooped down and kissed to her. "Then I have plenty for us to do."

"Oh, is that right?"

He stood abruptly and grabbed her hand.

"What are you doing?" she asked, laughing.

"We are getting in the hot tub." He walked backwards, guiding her along with him.

"I don't have a bathing suit."

"You won't need one." His grin widened.

They arrived near the covered tub that was sunk down in the patio.

"Seriously?" She reached up and tucked her hair behind her ear.

Karl closed the distance between them and tipped her chin up. "I'm very serious. If I get to have you here all night on this beautiful evening, then I want to spend it with you naked, in the tub while you ride me."

Nykee's breath caught in her throat. She swallowed hard and jerked her head in a nod.

"So, where are the towels?" she asked.

"Upstairs and to the left there's a closet. Grab us a few, and I'll turn the tub on and get your bag from the car."

Nykee didn't need to be told twice. She spun around and went inside. She loved everything about Karl's house. It had his touch to it, and it felt like a home and not a bachelor pad as she had originally expected. She would guess Billie had a hand in the decorations.

Nykee made her way upstairs and found the closet. She took out three fluffy towels and shut the door. She went into the bathroom and closed the door. She placed the towels down on the sink and stared at herself.

There were so many emotions running through her she didn't know what to think. When she had sat in that cell all those years ago, she had prayed for a better life. A happy one. Someone who would make her smile.

One thing she understood after going through therapy was that one person couldn't be responsible for her happiness. Only she was, but it helped to have someone in her life who inspired good emotions. She quickly used the facilities then went back downstairs carrying the towels. Her bag was sitting at the base of the stairs. She was glad she had decided to pack it. She opened it and snagged out a ponytail holder and slid it onto her wrist.

She arrived back outside and found Karl standing next to the bubbling hot tub in nothing but his boxer briefs. Her mouth grew dry at the perfect sight of him bending over. The muscles in his back rippled as he tested the water's temperature with his hand.

"I'm back," she announced.

He stood to his full height and turned to face her. Her gaze roamed his body, and she could barely move her attention away from the bulge in his shorts.

"Good. I was wondering what was taking so long." Using two fingers, he motioned for her to come to him.

Her feet moved before she could even think about it. He took the towels and placed them down on the floor near the tub.

He motioned to her clothes. "Those have got to go."

Nykee held his gaze while putting her hair in a bun on top of her head. She didn't want to risk getting her hair wet since she didn't have everything she would need to wash it if it got wet.

Her hands went to her shirt and pulled it over her head. Karl took it from her and dropped it on the pile of his clothes.

Nykee's heart rate increased while she continued.

Karl's eyes darkened as he silently watched her remove her clothing. She paused when she was in her panties and bra only.

Karl tugged her to him. Her body slammed against his. He swooped down and took her lips in a deep, passionate kiss. His hand went around her back and undid the clasp of her bra in a manner of seconds. Nykee melted against him. He controlled every part of the kiss. His hands shifted to her shoulders and pushed the straps down her arms. He stepped back, breaking the kiss. Her bra fell to the floor, but Nykee didn't care. Her heart was pounding, and her breaths were coming fast.

"Take my shorts off," Karl whispered. He stood still and waited for her.

Nykee bit her lip and held his heated gaze. There was a challenge in his eyes, as if he thought she wouldn't do it. She bit back a smirk and rested her fingers on the edge of his shorts. She hooked her thumb underneath the elastic and tugged on them.

She moved with the cotton material and knelt on the floor before him. His cock sprang free. She was eye level with the engorged shaft.

"Fuck," he muttered.

"What? I did what you told me to." She stared up at him innocently.

He kicked away the shorts still watching her. She

reached out and gripped the smooth cock that was so beautiful she just had to worship it.

Her lips closed around the mushroomed head. The sound of his inhaled breath brought a smile to her lips. She blinked and looked up at him while she swallowed as much of his length as she was able to.

"That you certainly did," he murmured.

His nostrils flared as moved her head. Her hand slid up and down his length in tandem with her mouth. His eyes fluttered closed and he allowed her to have her way with him.

His groan, the sexiest sound she'd ever heard, ripped through the air.

Nykee basked in the joy that it was she who was giving him pleasure.

The taste of him was divine. The saltiness of his desire leaked out the tip of his cock. She popped him out of her mouth and took her time running her tongue along the length of him. She traced the bulging vein along the underside of his member before returning to the head. She teased him by licking the drop of precum from his slit.

"Jesus," he muttered.

His hand rested on the back of her head just as she took him back inside her mouth. She felt herself growing wet and held back her whimper. Sucking his cock was turning her completely on. Her core clenched when he hit the back of her throat.

She instinctively swallowed, eliciting another groan from Karl.

Her eyes flicked up to him and caught him with his head thrown back. His hands gripped her bun and guided her head up and down on him. She cupped his scrotum and massaged the delicate sac. He hissed, his grip on her hair tightening. His abdomen rose and fell sharply while she continued her task at hand.

He had a large, beautiful cock that she didn't mind at all taking into her mouth.

What woman wouldn't want to please a man like Karl? He was everything she would imagine a man to be, and if she didn't know any better, she was already falling for him.

"Baby, we got to slow down," he rasped. He pulled on her bun until her mouth released him. "As much as I love what you are doing, this wasn't what I had planned."

"You can't plan out every little detail," she murmured. Her hand still gripped him at the base of his cock. She stroked him then placed a kiss to the tip of his cock.

"That is true, but one thing I won't accept is me

coming before you." He took her by her hand and helped her up.

Her heart leaped at his declaration.

Karl was a generous lover and always ensured she reached her peak.

He dragged her panties off and tossed them out of sight. He assisted her into the water and got in himself. He sank down and motioned for her to come to him.

Nykee didn't waste any time straddling him. Her body was strung tight, and her pussy ached to have him inside her.

They moved to each other, their mouths crashing together in a hard kiss. Karl wrapped an arm around her waist to hold her to him. Her breasts were crushed between them.

Karl's tongue demanded entrance into her mouth. He slipped inside and stroked her tongue. Nykee cupped his face, intent on drowning in the kiss. Karl's magic was weaving around her. Everything about him was perfect.

The way he kissed.

The way he treated her.

It was almost too good to be true.

If this was a dream, Nykee never wanted to wake up from this.

Karl's mouth left her lips and trailed along her

jawline and down to her neck. He left hot, open-mouthed kisses along the way. His large hands cupped her breasts and brought one to his mouth.

His cock pressed against her bottom. She rocked her hips, her pelvis seeking out his engorged member. Karl rolled her pebbled nipple in his mouth with his tongue.

The move sent a jolt of lightning to her core.

A whimper escaped her at the feeling of his cock brushing her bottom.

"Karl," she gasped.

"What is it, Nykee." He scraped his teeth along her sensitive little bud.

Her hands went to his shoulders, and her head dropped forward. Her body was on fire, and he was the only one who could meet the need growing inside her.

"Tell me what you need."

Her eyes fluttered open and met his.

"You."

"Then take me and put me where you need me," he rasped.

His hands squeezed her two mounds on her chest. She reached behind herself and took a hold of his cock. She lifted herself and nuzzled the blunt tip of him at her slick entrance. Water sloshed around them, escaping over the side of the tub, but neither of them paid it any attention.

They were lost in each other.

Nykee held her breath as she impaled herself on his length, taking him inside her slick core. A moan slipped from both of them once he was lodged completely in her. His hand slid down to her ass and cupped it.

Nykee leaned forward and rested her forehead against his. Karl was a large man, and he filled her up. Her inner walls screamed at being stretched so far, but she wouldn't complain. It felt so good, she never wanted him to pull out of her. He could remain buried inside her for an eternity for all she cared.

"Oh God," she groaned.

She rested her hands on the edge of the tub behind Karl. She inhaled sharply and rose before sliding back down his length. He hissed but didn't say a word. His hold on her tightened.

She repeated the motion, and this time, Karl helped lift her and forced her down while he thrust up, wedging his thickness into her. A cry tore from her at his brutal invasion.

She loved every second of it. He repeated it again, and she cried out.

"Nykee. You feel so good wrapped around me. I love how you fucking take me."

Nykee closed her eyes and held on for the ride. Karl's dirty talk was ensuring the heat for him climbed.

He took control of their lovemaking, guiding her up and down on his cock. He increased their rate, his hands digging into her flesh while he pounded away inside her. The water in the hot tub sloshed all around them, some of it escaping again.

And again, neither of them cared.

"Yes," she hissed.

Their breaths grew mingled as they moved together in synchrony. She rose, and he guided her down on him while he rose, too.

It was the perfect combination, driving his cock far into her. His strong arm wrapped around her, holding her down while he continued to plunge deep inside her.

Heat rushed through her. Nykee's body trembled uncontrollably as her orgasm coursed through her. Nykee held on to Karl, watching him lose himself.

Her lungs were robbed of air when her orgasm crashed into her. She cried out, her pussy tightening around him. It pulsed, milking his cock.

Their cries and shouts filled the air. They careened over the cliff into their simultaneous climaxes.

Karl tugged her face down to him and rested

their foreheads against each other. His semisoft cock was still lodged inside her.

"I don't know what you do to me." Karl panted.

Nykee's only response was a sigh. She could barely drag air into her lungs. She felt the same way. There was something about him that had her body responding in a crazy way. It was as if they were made for each other.

"Are you okay? I didn't hurt you, did I?"

"Only in a good way."

❧ 14 ☙

"And who is this we have here?" a loud boisterous voice rang out behind them.

Karl glanced over his shoulder and found his father's older brother standing behind them. He turned around with a wide grin. Nykee was glued to his hip, but he hadn't minded. He sensed she didn't do well with large crowds.

Not that he didn't want her at his side.

After their night at his house, he didn't want to let her out of his sight. They had stayed in the hot tub for about an hour then headed up to his bedroom afterwards. They hadn't dozed off until the wee hours in the morning.

He had taken advantage of having Nykee in his bed. There was something about waking up with her beside him this morning that had his dick ready to go. They were almost late to the cookout because he was barely able to keep his hands off her. Her soft brown skin had pulled him in, and before he knew it, he was sliding into her soft, silky channel.

Everything about this morning felt right.

He usually didn't have women spending the night at his house but felt as if she belonged there.

"Uncle Mitch. How the hell are you?" Karl released Nykee for a moment to greet his uncle with a huge bear hug.

Mitch Tanis lived a few hours north but always made sure he came down for the Tanis cookout.

"I'm doing well. You know me and your aunt Sarah wouldn't miss your mother's shindig for nothing in the world." His attention moved to Nykee.

Karl grinned and stepped back and wrapped an arm around her waist. She had been shy but was slowly opening up with his family.

"Uncle Mitch, I'd like for you to meet my girl-friend, Nykee Nash."

"She's such a pretty little thing. What does she see in your ugly mug?" Mitch stepped forward and held his hand out to Nykee who was grinning.

Karl tried to scowl at his uncle but fell short.

"Hello, darling. I'm this knucklehead's uncle. His father is my baby brother."

"Hello, sir. It's nice to meet you." Nykee giggled.

"There's no sir around here parts," Mitch sputtered. "You can call me Uncle Mitch just as this boy does."

"Thank you, sir—Uncle Mitch." Nykee nodded.

Karl wrapped his arm around her again, needing to feel her against him.

"You don't have a sister by chance, do you?" Mitch asked.

Karl rolled his eyes. His uncle and aunt were trying to get their boys hitched.

"I do, but she's happily married with three children," Nykee replied. There was a twinkle in her eye that he loved to see.

"Well, if this one messes up, I have a son that's better looking—"

"Hey, I'm right here," Karl cut his uncle off.

Mitch threw his head back with a hefty laugh pouring from him. His uncle was a jokester and loved busting his balls.

"You know I'm just playing with you." Mitch wiped the tears from his cheeks. He shook his head and tossed Nykee a wink.

"Well, maybe I'll keep that in mind just in case

this one acts up." Nykee nudged him in the side with her elbow.

Karl's mouth dropped open at her joke.

"I like this one." Mitch roared laughing. He patted Karl on the shoulder. "She's a keeper. Now let me find where my wife has disappeared to."

"Is Cam and Jase here?" Karl asked.

"Them boys of mine promised to show up. We'll see if they do." Mitch gave them a nod and headed off.

"Your family is so nice," Nykee said. She had a look of awe on her face.

Every person who he'd introduced her to was pleasant and made sure she felt welcomed. His family was a good group of people who were close-knit and loved to have fun. When anyone threw a party, they could always expect at least fifty people to show up.

"Are you enjoying yourself?" he asked. He dropped a kiss to the top of her head.

The sun was shining, and it was abnormally warm for a fall day. The family was spread out over the park. The basketball courts were full with kids playing, music pumped out of the large speakers spread around the area, while the scent of delicious barbecue floated through the air.

Billie had outdone herself again.

His gaze landed on a few familiar figures sitting together at a table.

"I am." Nykee reached up and popped a kiss to his chin.

"Come on. There's some people I need to speak with." He entwined their fingers together and towed her behind him. He headed over to the table where a few of the guys from the Blazing Eagle sat with their women. His grin spread wide as they drew closer. He hadn't seen them arrive. "Well, howdy, folks."

Rashad sat with Yani at his side. Stan with Nasia along with Wade and Joy. Greetings went around the table. Everyone stood and came around to him and Nykee. He quickly introduced her to everyone.

"Now I see why Karl hasn't been staying around for overtime lately." Wade chuckled. The middle Brooks brother grinned and jerked his chin toward Nykee.

"Her company is much better than grouchy cowboys," Karl shot back.

Nykee giggled and wrapped an arm around him.

"I'm sure I can find something to do with my time to allow Karl to stay on the ranch," she replied. That devious twinkle was back in her eyes.

"Not a chance." He pressed a kiss to her forehead before turning back to his friends. "Y'all having a good time?"

"We sure are. Your mom certainly knows how to throw a party." Rashad picked up his tall-neck beer and took a sip. He nodded in Billie's direction. "And the food is awesome."

"Gonna have to go work this off," Wade murmured.

"There is nothing for you to work off." Joy, his wife, elbowed him.

Karl shook his head at the two of them. It was interesting that they were together.

For as long as Karl had known Wade, he'd always heard that the rancher and Joy hated each other, and it dated back to childhood. Their families also had a rivalry that dated back generations, but it had been settled once Joy and Wade had fallen in love. Now they were married and had a kid.

"Nykee, you look familiar. Did you grow up here in Shady Springs?" Nasia asked. She tilted her head curiously as she stared at Nykee.

"I did." Nykee stiffened slightly.

Karl rubbed small circles on her torso to try to calm her. He took notice that whenever she spoke about the past, she withdrew slightly. Her muscles would go tense, and a strange expression always passed across her face. She threw up walls a mile high to avoid talking about her past. It frustrated Karl because he wasn't one to judge, but he swore he would be patient and wait for her to share things in her past with him.

"We graduated from high school the same year. I remember our senior year, we had first period together." Nasia smiled, apparently happy she remembered.

Karl got the sense that Nykee didn't really remember much from high school. He knew she'd run in the wrong crowds and got in trouble a lot.

"Nasia owns the Shady Bean Café," he said, trying to change the subject.

"Oh, wow. I love that little café," Nykee exclaimed. Her features brightened at the announcement. "I'm trying not to go in there every day just because I'm sure all the calories from your pastries will go to my hips."

"That's wonderful. Stan here is my test subject." She laughed and wrapped an arm around Stan's waist.

"And it is with much sacrifice of my body that I take one for the team," Stan joked.

"With as much as you work on that ranch, you have nothing to worry about." Nasia giggled.

"We're still waiting on the latest taste tests. I swear I think Stan is being selfish and keeping the goods for himself," Karl said.

"I don't know what you are talking about." Stan shook his head.

"Stan! Are you not taking the boxes I give you to the ranch?" Nasia scolded him.

Everyone laughed at Stan's expense while he sat there trying to make up excuses. It was nice to see his friend in a good, healthy relationship. Stan's ex-wife had done a number on him. She'd cheated on him with his best friend. It had left Stan a bitter man until he'd met Nasia.

"Are they putting up a badminton net?" Joy exclaimed.

They all turned to where she was pointing.

"Looks like it." Wade nodded.

"We've got to play." Joy bounced around with a grin spreading across her face. "How about a friendly game of guys against girls?"

"I'm down," Nasia said.

"Me, too." Yani giggled. She pushed at Rashad. "You're going down."

"Sounds like we don't have a choice." Rashad laughed. He tried to wrap an arm around Yani, but she pushed him away.

"Oh, no you don't. You are officially the enemy now." She went over to Joy and Nasia.

The girls turned to Nykee with welcoming smiles.

"You in?" Joy asked Nykee.

Each one of them had big puppy eyes watching Nykee who shrugged, a smile forming on her lips.

"Let's do this," Nykee said. She moved from his side and went over to the women.

"Welp, it looks like we're about to get our asses handed to us," Stan murmured.

"Like hell we are. Let's kick some ass." Rashad chuckled. "Yani is very competitive, and I'll never live it down if she beats me in this game. No mercy."

"Well, let's go." Karl watched Nykee as she smiled and spoke with the girls.

She glanced over her shoulder as if sensing him watching her. He tossed her a wink.

"Oh, none of that, Karl." Joy blocked his view of Nykee. "She's in good hands now. You go with the guys."

Karl laughed and turned to Rashad. He wrapped an arm around his shoulder and led the way over to the nets.

"Men, let's go!" he commanded. He felt good that the girls were trying to welcome Nykee. He wasn't worried about them. They would make her feel as one of the group.

❧

Nykee couldn't stop laughing. Their game of badminton was hilarious. They made up rules as they went along. It was four against four when Nykee thought the game either called for singles or doubles.

But it didn't matter.

They were having too much fun. They had gained an audience watching them that was split. Women cheered for the women, while the men backed up Karl and his friends.

"Nykee! Get it!" the girls screamed.

Nykee blinked and saw the white birdie was flying toward her. She swung her racket and connected, sending it back over the next.

She grinned and watched Karl dive for it. He missed and landed face-first on the grass.

"Yay!" Nykee screamed.

"We won!" Joy hollered, jumping up and down.

The girls rushed together, high-fiving and hugging each other. Nykee had to admit the girls were very welcoming and made her feel as if she had been part of their group for years.

Laughter and clapping went around from the spectators.

Groans and curses came from the men's side of the net. Nykee laughed and caught sight of Rashad helping Karl up from the ground.

"That was a kick-ass shot," Joy said. She patted Nykee on her shoulder.

"Thanks." Nykee exhaled, trying to catch her

breath. She didn't realize how physical one had to be just to play badminton. She was completely out of shape and was going to have to do something about it.

"I would say congratulations, but you girls were cheating the entire game." Rashad's lips were curved up into a grin.

"You shut your mouth, Rashad Mays." Yani snickered.

He ducked underneath the net and jogged over to her. She took off with a scream, but he caught her and lifted her off the ground.

Nykee smiled and turned back to see Karl headed her way. Her breath caught in her throat at the sight of his disheveled look. His hair was standing up on end, and grass stains were on the knees of his jeans. His smile lit up his face, and her heart stuttered.

She was going to be in trouble.

It would be too easy to fall for a man like Karl.

Hell, she might just be halfway there.

"That was one hell of a hit," he murmured. He pulled her into his embrace.

She dropped her racket and returned his hug.

"Thanks." She breathed in his scent and leaned into him. "Are you okay? It looks like you hit the ground hard."

"Nothing I haven't done before." He grinned.

"Why am I not surprised." She snorted.

The crowd that had been watching them was thinning out. Nykee stiffened when she caught sight of Deputy Griffen standing on the edge of the grass. His gaze was locked in on her.

"Karl, we hate to run, but we have to go," Wade said.

He and Joy walked arm in arm together and stopped before them.

"Thanks for coming. I appreciate it." Karl's arm tightened around her.

He and Wade discussed ranch business, and Nykee tuned it out.

"Make sure Karl works off this loss, girl." Joy winked at her.

"Of course. I'll think of something." Nykee drummed up a smile that she would.

The girls were very competitive. The shit-talking between each couple had been hilarious. Rashad and Yani were in deep conversation with Stan and Nasia. She had learned that the girls were close, as was Stan and Rashad. The girls grinning and the guys rolling their eyes.

Her gaze flicked over into the direction of the deputy. Her heart skipped a beat at the sight of him making his way to her. Behind him stood Deputy Pittman, taking in the park.

Nykee stiffened and tried to pull away from Karl. He turned to her with a frown until his gaze landed on Griffen. That frown morphed into a scowl. Nykee wasn't sure why he looked at the deputy the way he was.

"Hello, folks." The deputy tipped his hat at them.

His phony smile wasn't fooling Nykee. He wasn't coming over for a friendly chat.

He wanted something.

"Deputy. What brings you out this way?" Wade asked.

Karl's fingers drew little circles on her side. It helped calmed her nerves, but at the moment there was a sour taste in her mouth. She didn't trust Griffen at all.

"Oh, you know, police business. Investigating the string of robberies that have picked up here in town," Griffen said.

"I've heard about that. Got any leads to who it could be?" Wade asked.

"I have my theories." Griffen chuckled. He turned his gaze to Nykee. "Miss Nash, may I have a word with you?"

Nykee didn't want to cause a scene. Wade and Joy eyed her curiously. This was embarrassing. Of all times of day, he just had to corner her at a function where there was a large crowd.

"Let's move over to where we can have some privacy," Karl replied. All of the smiles and joking was gone from his face. He jerked his chin in a direction where no one was near.

"But of course." The deputy nodded.

"Everything good, Karl?" Wade asked. He didn't look as if he trusted the situation. He narrowed his eyes on them.

"We're good. I'll talk with you later," Karl said over his shoulder. He took Nykee's hand and entwined their fingers together.

She glanced over at him and took in his stern expression. Nykee couldn't remember a time where he'd appeared this serious. They walked a little ways away in silence to where no one would be able to hear their conversation. Pittman trailed behind them.

Yeah, something was up with them.

The stroll gave Nykee her confidence back. There was no reason for the deputy to be asking to speak with her. She hadn't done anything wrong and sure wasn't involved in any robberies. They arrived next at a tree that offered plenty of shade from the sun that was high.

"What can we do for you?" Nykee asked.

Karl tightened his grip on her. She didn't take her eyes off Griffen while she waited for his reply.

"Nykee, we need you to come down to the station for some questioning." Griffen leveled her with a stern gaze.

"Am I being arrested?" she asked.

"What is this about?" Karl demanded.

"Karl, I mean this with as much respect as I can give, but this isn't of your concern," Griffen said.

"Like hell it isn't. You keep harassing my girlfriend, and I'm making it my business," Karl snapped.

Nykee had to push down her excitement at his fierce protective nature. Unfortunately, she was used to fighting her own battles.

"If I'm not under arrest, then I'm not going anywhere with you." Nykee shook her head. There was no way in hell she was going with them for any conversation without a lawyer. She knew people who had gone to prison for saying the wrong thing.

"Now, Miss Nash, you don't have to be so dramatic. We just need to clear some things up." Griffen sniffed. He rested his hands on his utility belt.

Nykee instinctively took a step back.

"You heard what she said. She's not going anywhere with you," Karl growled.

"Again, Karl, this is none of your business," Griffen barked. He focused back on Nykee and flipped the snap on where he kept his handcuffs. "Well, if you want to be so darn stubborn, then we'll do it your way. It's been a long time since I've put cuffs on you."

Nykee stared him down, refusing to budge. She had no worries about anything. Karl stepped in front of her.

"Move, Karl," Pittman said from behind them.

Griffen walked over to Nykee with a grin. "Nykee Nash, you are under arrest."

Almost out of habit, her hands moved to behind her back. She had spent many years having the cold clamps on her wrists. She blocked out the words that Griffen spoke while he read her the Miranda rights. The familiar feeing of the steel around her skin took her back to a place she thought she had left behind.

"She didn't do anything," Karl hollered.

Nykee dropped her gaze to her feet, not wanting to see his expression.

"We'll see about that," Griffen snarled.

"I want my lawyer," Nykee announced. It would be the only words she'd utter until she spoke with her council. Anything else, they would definitely use against her. So until she spoke with her long-time lawyer, she wasn't going to open her mouth and say anything else.

"But you're innocent. Why would you need your

lawyer?" Griffen chuckled and guided her down the slope of the small hill they had walked up. "All we wanted to do was chat."

"I want my lawyer," she repeated. She stared down at her feet until they arrived near the party. A lump formed in her throat as she was led away through the cookout. She felt eyes on her and knew if she looked up it would kill her to see their expressions.

"Don't worry about anything, baby. I'll call whoever you need me to call," Karl said, marching along with them.

She kept her eyes trained on the back of Pittman's feet since he was in front of her. Nykee didn't respond to Karl. It hurt too much for him to see her like this. This wasn't the type of life she'd want for him. He was a good guy and deserved a woman who the police weren't prejudiced against.

"Don't say a thing. I'll get a hold of your parents," Karl said.

She jerked her head in a nod. Her father would contact her lawyer. They took her over to one of the patrol cars and opened the back door.

"Watch your head, Miss Nash," Pittman said.

Griffen guided her head down and helped her into the car. She kept her eyes trained on her lap and blocked out everything else.

She jerked at the slam of the door. Her sight grew blurry from the unshed tears that threatened to spill.

Everything was too good to be true. She had doubted everything but tried to enjoy it all before it came crashing down around her.

Nykee had hoped she was finally going to live her full life, but she had ignored one thing she knew.

Trouble always followed her.

"You really aren't going to talk, are you?" Griffen stared across the table at her.

Nykee kept her mouth shut. The only words she had uttered were the same ones she had been saying for the last twenty minutes. Griffen thought he would crack her and break her down to where she would cooperate.

But the funny thing was, he was barking up the wrong tree.

He was so set on laying the blame on her for whatever was going on that he couldn't even see it. She made a note to start watching the news more often so she would know what was going on in their small town. They kept mentioning break-ins and robberies, but she had no clue what they were talking about.

Breaking into people's homes were things she'd done when she'd been a teenager. Once she was in with Foster and made officially his woman, petty theft was a thing of the past.

Nykee guessed there was a downside of staying to herself. She didn't hear the latest gossip.

"I want my phone call." She kept her voice low and her eyes steady on her hands that were resting on the table. Her gaze was locked on the silver cuffs encircling her wrists. It had been three years since she'd felt the weight of cold hard steel against her skin.

When she'd walked out of Colorado Women's Prison, she had vowed she would never wear them again.

Now here she was, innocent yet detained.

She wasn't going to lose her cool or anything. She was going to wait patiently until they led her to a phone where she could call her lawyer.

Griffen sat back in his chair and sighed. He ran a hand along his jaw and glared at her.

"Fine. You can have your phone call." He stood and walked over to the door to the small interrogation room and waved someone in. "Take her so she may make her phone call."

An officer who appeared a few years younger than

Nykee joined her. Griffen gave her one last look before disappearing from the room.

The young cop walked over and unhooked her cuffs from the table. She stood and wished he would have removed them from around her wrists, but that wouldn't happen quite yet.

"Come with me." He cupped her elbow and led her from the room.

They walked down a short hall and stepped into a private room with a phone on the wall. A single chair rested near the phone. She entered and made a beeline for the phone.

He paused inside the room with his hand on the door. "Open the door when you are done."

She jerked her head in a nod and waited for him to close the door. Once she was alone, she sat in the chair and picked up the phone.

Luckily, she had her lawyer's cell number memorized.

One ring, and a familiar voice answered.

"Cain Moss."

"Mr. Moss, it's Nykee Nash," she announced. Her lawyer had been a good one. He had fought so hard for her. The state had been trying to throw time at her like they had Foster. She had been lucky to do the small amount of time she had. With any other lawyer, she might have been given twenty-plus years along with Foster. But Mr. Moss was relentless, and her term had been much smaller.

"Well, I'll be damned. I'm going to assume this isn't a social call and you're not just checking up on me," he joked. Mr. Moss always did reserve a little humor to help settle her nerves.

"I wish I could say that it was." Nykee sighed. She closed her eyes and settled back in her chair. Emotions swirled around in her chest, but she pushed them down. Now wasn't the time to cry. She honestly didn't know why Griffen had it out for her. Was it because of her background only?

If that was the case, then he was a lazy police officer.

Nykee inhaled slowly. Mr. Moss would get her freed immediately. She was confident in his abilities.

"So, tell me what's going on." Mr. Moss's voice grew serious, all joking put aside.

She briefly went through what had been going on the last few weeks and everything leading up to her arrest. He remained quiet, asking a question or two. When she was done, she waited.

"They don't have any reason to hold you, much less arrest you."

Relief filled Nykee.

This was just what she wanted to hear.

"I know they don't."

"You did good by not saying anything."

"Well, I have the best lawyer around to teach me." She chuckled. When she was younger, she was a hothead and didn't know how to keep her mouth shut. Thanks to Mr. Moss, it was he who taught her how to remain cool and collected. There were ways police were trained to interact with people that could lead them to unknowingly get themselves into trouble.

"Don't worry about this, Nykee. I'll call and see what their bogus charges are. Can you just sit tight for a little bit?" he asked.

"Yeah, I can, but don't let it take too long," she said. Goosebumps appeared on her skin at the thought of going back into the holding cells.

"Don't worry. You won't be spending the night."

"Thank you," she whispered. She ended the call, and Nykee hung up the phone. She sat there for a moment and tried to will the tears that blurred her vision to go away. She didn't want any of the deputies to see her at a weak point.

Her chest tightened at the thought of Karl. He had to see her be hounded by the police and arrested. He had walked along with her while she'd been led to the cruiser. His voice was frantic as he'd promised to do something to help her.

Her heart stuttered at the thought of what she needed to do.

She was going to have to push him away. As much as she didn't want to, she couldn't be involved with him. Her stomach cramped at the thought of no longer seeing him. She loved the scent of him, his warm eyes, his strong embrace, and his addictive kisses.

He deserved to find a woman who wasn't complicated.

Nykee had known this was all too good to be true. There was something that had plagued her, a doubt in the back of her mind, that they wouldn't work out.

She bit back a sob.

Happiness apparently wasn't in the cards for her.

Nykee had come to the realization that she may be single for the rest of her life before she'd met Karl. He gave her everything she had craved, and she had wanted to hold on to it.

But she wanted to ensure Karl could lead a life of happiness—just not with her.

He would move on and find a woman who was better suited for him. Someone who didn't have a criminal past.

She stood from the chair and moved over to the

door. She opened it and peeked her head out. The young officer stood a few feet away.

"I'm done," she announced.

"Come with me, Ms. Nash." He walked over to her and guided her through another door at the end of the hall. She hadn't caught his name, but he appeared nicer than Griffen and Pittman.

"Where are you taking me?" She sniffed.

It had been a few years, but her old habits came back strong. Instinctively, she kept her head down, voice low. It was something she had learned to do to try not to attract any attention from the guards. Many of them had considered her pretty and were willing to overlook a few things for a price. There were plenty of women she knew who would take the correctional officers up on their offers, but not Nykee.

She had to have some pride left.

In prison, she hadn't controlled any part of her life. They'd told her when to sleep, eat, and shower. She'd gone by the prison's schedule. When she'd been released, it was hard for her to break that schedule.

Being able to decide when to take a shower had become a luxury. Or just to get up and go where she wanted were things she had always taken for granted.

"To a holding cell."

Nykee grew silent. She completely shut down all

her thoughts and emotions. She wasn't going into a prison, but the thought of being detained behind bars did something to her. She had always promised herself she would never return, but for some reason, here she was.

They arrived in holding cell area. There were separate cells, and the women and men were kept separate. Across the hall from where he led her, a figure lay out on the bench. He must be a drunk sleeping off the alcohol. She wrinkled her nose at the stench coming from the man.

The bars squeaked as the cop opened the door.

"Please turn towards me," the officer instructed.

Nykee faced him, and her gaze landed on his last name embroidered on his shirt.

Officer Holmes.

He took his key and inserted it into the steel chain's lock.

"Thank you," she murmured. The cuffs fell away from her skin. She automatically massaged her wrists while she walked into the cold cell.

She jerked at the sound of it slamming shut. She turned and caught Holmes's eyes before he turned and strode away.

Pity was what she saw.

He, too, assumed she was guilty of crimes she had not committed. They were all the same.

Nykee blew out a deep breath and took a seat on the bench along the wall. She eyed the area, and tremors racked her body.

You won't be spending the night.

Moss's words echoed through her head. That was the only reason she wasn't growing hysterical. Leaning her head back against the stone wall, she tried to calm down her racing heart. She would have to trust Mr. Moss.

Unsure of how much time she was going to spend in the tiny cell, she began to think of how she would break things off with Karl and how she would move on with a broken heart.

৩৩

"WHAT DO YOU MEAN I CAN'T SEE HER?" KARL growled. He leaned against the counter and stared at the man sitting behind the desk.

He'd been waiting for what seemed to be hours. The first time he'd demanded to see Nykee, he was given the excuse they were processing her.

Now, he couldn't see her at all?

"Sir, there's nothing I can do at the moment. If you are not her council, then I can't let you back there." Officer Turner returned Karl's stare with a glare of his own. He motioned to the chairs in the waiting area. "What you can do for now is have a seat and wait."

Karl released a curse and stalked over to the other side of the room. He was too wired to sit down. He had finally found the number to Nykee's parents and had given her father a call.

The call had been short and to the point. The older man didn't question Karl at all once he'd told him that Nykee had been taken into custody.

The door swung open, and a handsome African-American couple entered the station. Karl took one look at them and immediately knew this was Nykee's parents. The older gentleman was tall, bald, and dressed in a short-sleeved button-down shirt and jeans. His skin was the same color as Nykee's while her mother was a shade lighter, but she was the exact image of Nykee only older with strands of gray woven throughout her hair.

"Mr. and Mrs. Nash." Karl stepped forward.

The couple paused and turned to him. He straightened to his full height as they took him in. He wasn't sure what they were expecting, but their expressions were unreadable. Nykee had spoken much about her family. He knew they were close-knit and they'd had conversations about him meeting them. Karl hated that the first time he met her parents was at the police station.

"I'm Karl Tanis. I was the one who called you." He walked over to them with his hand outstretched.

"Thanks for calling, Karl. You can call me Lou, and this is my wife, Pearlina." Lou took his hand in a firm shake. The older man sized him up quickly before turning to his wife.

"Hello, ma'am." Karl took Pearlina's hand next.

She offered him a warm smile, even though it didn't quite meet her eyes. There was tension in the air, and Karl was sure his call hadn't been expected.

"It's nice to meet you, Karl. Our other daughter, Shara, has clued us in on who you are, even though Nykee has kept you practically all to herself." She stepped back and stood beside her husband.

Karl's lips tilted up. That sounded like Nykee. She was still opening up to the fact that he wanted her. He had been shocked she had admitted to her sister that they were in a relationship. Her claiming she had 'locked him down' did something for his ego.

"I'm sorry we had to meet under these circumstances," Karl began. He had to beat down his anger. The police had their sights on Nykee and were convinced she had committee some crazy crime. He just wanted to see her, talk with her, and make sure she was okay. He glanced over at the officer at the desk then turned back to Nykee's parents. "They won't let me see her or talk to her. I don't even know what's going on."

"I'll get to the bottom of this." Lou's lips pressed together in a hard line. He walked over to the desk and spoke quietly with the officer.

"What happened, Karl?" Pearlina asked.

Air escaped him as he rotated back to her. Concern lined her face, and he really didn't have much information. He started at the beginning. He shared with her the times the deputies had been approaching Nykee up until the cookout. By the time he'd finished the story, Lou had rejoined them.

"Are they talking about the robberies that they've been mentioning on the news?" Pearlina turned to her husband who wrapped an arm around her waist.

"I'm not sure, ma'am. I haven't really been watching the news." Karl scratched his head. Maybe he should have been, but he had never been one to watch the news. He mainly caught the weather on an app on his phone. Working on a ranch left little time for him to do anything once he got home but shower, eat, and sleep before he was up again and off to work.

"We're not sure how much Nykee has shared with you, but I can tell you one thing. My daughter hasn't robbed anyone since she was sixteen years old." Lou glanced over at the door that opened.

If that was the case, then why was Griffen determined to pin these crimes on her? Something didn't smell right.

"Mr. Nash, you can come on back." Griffen stood at the door. His gaze landed on Karl for a moment then shifted back to the Nashes.

"I'll be right back, my dear. You stay here." Lou pressed a kiss to Pearlina's forehead.

"I'll sit out here with her," Karl said. He held out his arm for Nykee's mother.

She took it and allowed him to escort her over to a chair.

Lou and the deputy disappeared through the door. Karl watched it slowly close before settling down into the chair next to Pearlina. He blew out a deep breath. At least someone would be allowed to go back there and see Nykee. He was worried about her. When they had led her away to the squad car, she wouldn't look at him. She had kept her eyes down and hadn't said much. The expression on her face had practically brought him to his knees. He'd felt helpless when they had driven away with her.

She didn't belong in a cage.

She belonged in his arms.

"You care for her, don't you?" Pearlina's soft voice broke through his thoughts.

It was tearing him up that he couldn't see or hold her. He was sure she was scared and pissed off at the same time. That was his Nykee. She may appear quiet, but he could always sense a little firecracker in her. Those eyes of hers were very giving and showed off her emotions.

Memories of the night before where they had made love in his hot tub came to mind. He loved watching her as she reached her peak on his cock.

He cleared his throat and reared in the images from last night. He shouldn't be remembering her screaming on his cock while sitting next to her mother. He flicked his gaze to Pearlina and found her watching him.

He jerked his head in a nod.

"Yes, ma'am. I do."

"Daddy." Nykee stood from her perch on the bench. She had started dozing off while waiting for someone to come get her out of this cell. Hearing footsteps, she had opened her eyes. The sight of her father standing outside the bars brought tears to her eyes.

She held them back once she saw he wasn't alone.

Griffen stood next to her father.

"I'll give you two a few minutes." Griffen nodded to her father before walking away, leaving them alone.

Nykee walked over to her bars. She wished they weren't in the way. She needed to feel her father's arms around her.

Louvell Nash looked every one of his sixty-two years. He was a tall man, well over six feet. He'd lost most of his hair in his early forties, blaming it on his children. There were plenty of photos around the house with him and his full head of hair. He had been so proud of his afro he'd worn back in the seventies. He and her brother resembled each other. His warm brown skin was golden, as if touched by the sun. He must have been hitting the golf greens more than he let on.

Lou sighed and stared at her without saying a word.

Nykee blinked back the tears. One escaped and ran down her cheek. She used the back of her hand to wipe it away. She had always been a daddy's girl. When she was a young child, she'd doted on her father. In her eyes, he was the best father in the world. He had worked hard to make sure she and her siblings didn't go without. They weren't rich by any means, but they had everything they needed.

He spoiled her rotten, and she had been ashamed of the woman she had grown up to be. It had taken a few years for her to realize that no matter what, her father would always love her.

She had the proof. He'd stood by her through everything she had done wrong in life. He and her mother had never given up on her. Each court hearing, they were there. When she'd come home, bruises covering her body, they'd welcomed her.

Nykee didn't know what she had done to deserve such parents, but she was thankful for them. When she had finally woken up and wanted a better life for herself, they were right there.

"I didn't do it, Daddy."

"I know, pumpkin."

She gripped the bars and leaned her forehead against the cold metal. She had vowed her father would never see her in a cage again. It had torn him apart all the times in her past when she had been arrested.

"I have to get out of here," she whispered. Her hands shook as tiny tendrils of fear crept inside her. Mr. Moss had said there was nothing for her to worry about, but that still didn't remove the little shred of worry.

"And you will. I spoke with Mr. Moss on the way here. He's working now to get you out. It shouldn't be too much longer." Her father's warm hands covered hers.

She glanced up at him and bit back another sob.

There was no judgement in his eyes.

Only love.

"Why have you never given up on me?" she whispered. This was something Nykee didn't know the answer to. She had spent many nights thanking the man above for the support and love of her family. It was astonishing that her parents had stuck by her side through all of the years. She wouldn't have blamed them for leaving her in that cell or denying her collect calls when she'd had a moment to phone home from prison.

"You are my daughter." Lou's eyes grew misty. A sad smile appeared on his lips while he held her gaze. "There is nothing you could do that would stop me from loving you. Until there is no more breath left in my body, I will always be there for you, and when I'm dead and gone, I'll still be looking down over you from Heaven."

Nykee's tears trailed down her cheeks.

"I love you, Daddy." Her voice was barely audible. It took everything she had to not sob aloud. She inhaled deeply and tried to rein in her emotions. Crying wasn't going to solve anything.

"And I you, baby. Now these deputies are going to have to answer for arresting you. Mr. Moss said that what they arrested you for was made up and he'll have you out of here soon. Just hang on, baby."

"I am." She shuddered and closed her eyes.

"And who is this Karl fellow? He called me and told me what happened." Her father leveled her with his gaze.

She swallowed hard and suddenly felt all of fourteen again when she'd had her first boyfriend. Her father hadn't liked the notion of his girls dating. She remembered him yelling that fourteen was too young to be having boyfriends.

She lowered her head, her cheeks warming.

Karl had called her father. He was probably going crazy out there with worry.

"He was my boyfriend," she said. She coughed slightly and cleared her throat.

"Was?" Her father's eyebrows rose sharply. He brushed the back of her fingers with his. "Why past tense? He's out there worried sick about you."

"I can't have him see me like this, Daddy." She shook her head. She closed her eyes briefly. Her mind was made up. She was going to have to break it off with him.

"Are you ashamed of your past?" her father asked quietly.

"He knows about it," she said. Nykee wasn't going to tell her father that she hadn't told Karl everything. And was she ashamed of her past?

She was.

There was nothing she could do to change it. She just couldn't bear the thought of the look of disgust on his face if she told him everything she had done. There were some things that even her family was unaware of. Things that no father should have to hear his daughter had done.

Foster had used her to get what he wanted.

And she had been foolish enough to let him. Everything she had done for him had been because she'd loved him. His success was her success. She held the coveted status as his girlfriend.

Never his wife.

Marriage had never been a subject they'd approached. Children, she had decided not long after their relationship began that she didn't want to risk having any with him. She'd immediately got on the birth control shot to ensure she wouldn't get accidentally pregnant.

Foster had said he wasn't quite ready for children. He wanted to focus on building his empire.

And after seeing his true nature, she was relieved she had made the decision she had made.

"So you just going to cut him because the deputies made a mistake arresting you?" her father asked.

"It's just not about today," she snapped. Nykee pushed off the bars and took a few steps away. She shoved her hair back away from her face. She inhaled sharply and blew out the air. Nykee turned and walked back to the bars. "Do you know how it feels to have your past thrown into your face constantly? No matter what I've done to try to build myself up, create a new life for myself, there is always someone wanting to remind me of where I've come from. All people see when they look at me is a criminal—"

"Not that boy out there," her father quietly interjected. He ran a hand along his face and held on to the bars. He leveled her with his gaze. "That man, I should say, cares about you. In the few minutes I've spent with him, I can see that. Don't push him away."

Nykee was shocked by his admission. Her father was normally conservative when it came to the men she and her sister had dated. It had taken him a few months to warm up to Rick when he and Shara was dating.

Nykee blinked and shook her head.

"My mind is made up," she responded. She wrapped her arms around her waist and held on to herself. There was a sharp pain in her chest. The intensity grew with each deep breath she took. Nykee would have to accept the fact that she was destined to be alone for the rest of her life.

But she hadn't planned to be completely alone. She was supposed to be searching for a dog to adopt and now she would get back to her search. Her future puppy would be her companion.

Get back to the life she had been setting up for herself.

"Then who will tell him?" her father asked.

She turned to him.

It was going to be hard, but she would have to let him down in person. She couldn't do it by phone.

"I will, but not today. Can you just tell him to go home?" She knew she was being a coward, but she needed more time.

Her father pressed his lips in a hard line, his gaze narrowed on her. It was evident he didn't want to do her dirty work, but she needed him to.

"Nykee—"

"I just need more time. Please, Daddy." Her voice dropped to a whisper. Her heart was already breaking, and she needed to get herself together before she had this conversation with Karl. He was a great guy and deserved so much more than she could give him.

"Fine. I'll tell him it will be a while and that you will call him." Her father backed away from the bars.

She knew she would be able to count on her father.

"It won't be too much longer. Deputy Griffen said they are working on your release now."

Nykee nodded and sat back down on the bench. She rested her elbows on her knees with her face in her hands. It wasn't until she heard her father's footsteps disappear that she allowed the tears to fall.

They burned trails down her skin as she thought

of everything she was giving up. Her shoulders shook as she held back the sobs.

This was the right thing to do. She was convinced of it.

If it was, then why did she feel as if her whole world was crumbling down around her?

❧

"IS THAT ALL YOU ARE GOING TO EAT?" PEARLINA glanced over at Nykee.

Nykee looked down at her soup and saw she had only eaten half of it. She had finally been released; all the bogus charges were dropped. Again, they had nothing on her, and Deputy Griffen knew it.

"I had eaten at the cookout I was at earlier," she said. There was so much food, there was no way she was going to avoid it. The scent of barbecue had filled the air. Billie had gone out of her way to ensure that everyone had enough to eat. Nykee had planned to go back for seconds but never had the chance.

"But that was hours ago. It's late and you need to eat."

Her mother's concern made her feel bad, but she truly didn't have an appetite. Her sandwich that went along with the soup had remained untouched.

"Leave her be, Pearl." Lou wiped his mouth with

his napkin. He eyed her then waved down the waitress. "She can just take it home and eat it later."

Nykee pushed the rest of her food away. She
stared out the window of the Farmhouse Diner. Her
parents had insisted on feeding her before they took
her home. The street was bustling with people
walking along the sidewalk. It was Saturday night,
and many of the townspeople would be hitting the
local bars and restaurants. The Farmhouse Diner was
packed. It was one of the popular restaurants. Her
parents were frequent customers at the establishment.

"Why don't you come stay with us tonight?"
Pearlina asked.

"I'll be fine. I just want to take a hot shower and
climb into my bed," Nykee murmured. It was a
tempting offer, but Nykee didn't think she would be
good company. She was in a sour mood and just
wanted to be alone. Her parents were worried about
her, it was easy to see. But she would be okay. She
would just need some time.

When she had been released from prison, she had
been withdrawn, unsure where she would fit in now
that she was back in Shady Springs. It had taken her
a while before she'd found her way. The people
sitting across from her with love in their eyes were
right there with her.

Just as they always were.

"Nothing wrong with that. I doubt she wants to sleep in the twin beds we put in her old room." Her father chuckled. Once her siblings started having children, her parents had redecorated their old rooms to accommodate the grandkids who loved spending the night.

The waitress came over with the check and containers for them to take their leftovers home. Nykee boxed up her food while her father took care of paying for their meal. Nykee followed her parents out of the diner while carrying her small bag.

She kept her eyes averted from those she passed. She could feel eyes on her. Everyone talked in Shady Springs.

Once in the car, her mother turned to look at her. Nykee offered her a small smile. There was no doubt Pearlina Nash was worried about her. She was always stressing over her children. It didn't matter that they were grown, Pearlina was a momma bear when it came to Nykee and her siblings.

"You should come and stay with us, honey. I really don't want you by yourself." Pearlina frowned. The woman was going to keep pressing until she got her way.

"Pearl, leave the girl alone. She's old enough to

make her own decisions." Lou sighed. He reached over and took his wife's hand.

Nykee settled in the back seat of their sedan. The love for her parents had gotten her through hard times.

"I'm fine, Mom. If I wasn't, I'd let you know." She turned her gaze to the scenery while it passed by. She planned to take a hot shower to wash the grime from the jail cell from her. She'd been in worse cells before, but just being in one again left her feeling unclean and dirty.

Once she got a good night's sleep, she think of Karl. It was going to tear her in two to break away from him. She was going to have to try to erase him from her mind, but she had a funny feeling that he was going to be hard to forget.

Frustration gripped Karl. He had been sitting with Mrs. Nash when Nykee's father had returned from his visit with her. Karl's heart had just about stopped when the elder man had come to him.

"It's going to be a long night, Karl. Why don't you go home." Lou sighed. He slid his hands into his pockets.

If it was possible, Karl would say the man had aged significantly since seeing Nykee. The eyes that settled on Karl were haunted and had a deep pain in them.

"I can wait for her," Karl replied. He stood, dread settling in the pits of his stomach. Something was wrong. "I don't want to leave her."

"What is it, Lou?" Pearlina joined them.

Her husband glanced at her before turning back to Karl.

His face softened. He reached out and rested a hand on Karl's shoulder.

"Karl, I'm just going to be straightforward. Nykee doesn't want to see you right now."

The small waiting room was deathly silent. The only sound was Pearlina murmuring something like a prayer of sorts.

Karl's lungs seized. He studied the man's eyes and saw the truth in them. Even a smidge of pity. He blinked and glanced away. He wasn't sure what to think of this. Why wouldn't she want to him here? Didn't she know that he cared for her?

"But, why?" He thanked the heavens above that his voice remained steady. He just couldn't fathom that she would push him away, but the memory of her when they'd first met came to mind. She had been guarded, wary even. She kept to herself, afraid of how people would think of her. The world could be cruel, and people judged her constantly off of her past.

Karl ran his fingers through his hair and blew out a deep breath.

"I'm not going anywhere." He stood to his full height and leveled Lou with a stern gaze. She wasn't going to walk away so easily. From the moment they'd met, he'd known she was special. She was someone he wanted to be with. The thought of forever with her had his heart pumping.

Whatever Lou saw in him made him nod, a satisfied look crossing his face.

"Just give her time, son." Lou squeezed his shoulder before releasing him. "She's stubborn like her mother—"

"Lou Nash," Pearlina gasped. She nudged him with her elbow, but a small smile appeared on her lips.

Lou slipped an arm around her waist and brought her flush against him. The love shining from his eyes was apparent.

"These Nash women are very stubborn and independent. Take it from me, son. Give her a little room and time. She'll come around."

Karl had given her a little time. A couple of hours should have been sufficient enough. His truck was parked a few doors down. He was able to see her drive and the front door from where he was. Was he sure she was coming home tonight?

No.

But if she didn't, he was prepared to come by her house every day if he had to or even go to her shop. She wasn't going to avoid him. He wasn't going to allow her to. The longer he'd had time to sit and think about the situation, he knew what she was doing.

Griffen had gotten into her head.

And because of this, she was going to try to push

him away. The men she'd been involved with had been shit. He'd done something he wasn't proud of while waiting in the truck.

He'd Googled her.

What he'd found was shocking.

Nykee had definitely gotten involved with the wrong crowd. Her name was attached to that of a high-profile drug king pin of Colorado. Karl had sat frozen while he'd read countless stories covering their trial. The cold, hard woman they'd painted couldn't be his woman—the girlfriend of a notorious criminal.

This Foster Moss had been tied into drugs, prostitution, and anything illegal. There were countless pictures of Nykee alongside him from old social media posts that the news shared. One picture caught his attention.

Nykee's mug shot.

The woman photographed looked like Nykee, but the eyes that stared back at him were soulless, lifeless, and held no emotion. She was alive but barely living.

It wasn't the same woman whose smile lit up the room or whose laugh was infectious.

He knew Nykee. She had come a long way and deserved a second chance. He didn't care about her past. She was a good woman who had made something of herself. It took a strong person to get past what she'd gone through and forge ahead in life. He respected how she had taken back her life.

This was who he had come to know.

Who he had come to love.

Karl paused.

Did he truly love Nykee? He did. There was no doubt about it. He had opened himself to her from the first moment he had laid his eyes on her, and she had captured his heart.

He was going to fight for her.

Beside her family, no one else sided with her, believed in her, and he was going to make her see that she couldn't just send her father to get rid of him. He wasn't going anywhere. She may be stubborn, but she didn't realize how bullheaded he could be.

A car traveling down the road caught his attention. He held his breath as he watched it turn into Nykee's driveway. The car sat idle for a few minutes before the back door opened. Nykee exited the vehicle and walked to her front door. She unlocked it and turned around to wave to her parents before disappearing into the home. The car waited until she shut the door then backed out and drove away.

Karl drove into her driveway and parked. His heart pounded away thinking of what he would say to her. In reality, he just wanted to hold her and ensure that she understood something like this wasn't going to scare him away.

He got out and stalked to the house. He jogged up the stairs and opened the screen door. He rang the doorbell impatiently. He rested his hands along the frame and waited. He drew in a deep breath and attempted to get his emotions together. He wanted to shake some sense into Nykee, but that wouldn't help anything.

Footsteps padded toward him. He grew tense, ready to force his way into her home the minute she cracked open the door. Karl stared into the peephole and felt Nykee on the other side of the door. The lock sounded, and the door opened slightly.

"What are you doing here, Karl?" Nykee's wide eyes met his through the crack.

He pushed his way into the house and slammed the door behind him.

"You sent your father to get rid of me?" he rasped. He couldn't help the emotions swirling around in him. The thought of being separated from her was overwhelming. He wasn't going to leave her alone.

She stepped back away from him, her eyes wide.

"Yes, I didn't want you to see me like that," she cried out.

He reached out and snagged her wrist and brought her to him. She resisted, but he overpowered her. She slammed into him. He cupped her cheeks and forced her to look at him. Tears spilled down her face. The tortured expression in her eyes just about brought him to his knees.

She was suffering internally.

Alone.

"Do you think seeing you like that was going to change how I feel about you?" He softened inside and wiped the wetness from her skin. He rested his forehead on hers and inhaled her scent. The light floral perfume met him. He dragged it in and exhaled. "It doesn't. I'm not going anywhere. I'm going to be right here by your side. Lean on me, babe. I got you."

Nykee's body slumped into him. He wrapped his arms around her. Her body was racked with sobs. His heart ripped in two at the sound of her cries. He just held her, running his hand along her back and whispering sweet nothings. He pressed his lips to the top of her head and just held on to her.

Karl lost track of time and didn't know how long they had stood there, but he didn't care. All that mattered was that Nykee knew she wouldn't have to face anything alone ever again. Her sobs finally quieted, and he had the full weight of her against him.

Karl didn't say a word but bent down and lifted her in his arms. He carried her through the house until he arrived at her bathroom. He stepped in and placed her on her feet. Her body slid along his. Karl ignored how well they fit together. This was not the time to take notice of her curvy frame. She needed him at the moment, and he was going to take care of her.

She stood still while he started the water running. He turned back to her and found her staring off into space. Her shoulders were slumped, tears marred her smooth skin, and her bottom lip trembled. He slowly removed her clothes, dropping them into a neat pile on the floor. He glanced at her hair then caught sight of her shower cap.

He snagged it and placed it on her head gently, scooping up her hair and sliding it inside. He stepped back and quickly shucked his clothes off. He guided her over to the shower and helped her in. He faced her to allow the warm water to run along her back. She rested her forehead against his chest and stood still.

Nykee drew in a shaky breath.

For a moment neither of them moved. The water slid along their skin while the steam filled the air.

Karl reached for her loofah and shower gel and began washing. He took his time bathing her.

Nykee stood there and allowed him to take care of her. It was apparent she never allowed anyone to see her at her low point. A slight pain appeared in his chest. How long had she suffered alone? Even though she had her family, she hid her true emotions from them.

He didn't want her to ever go through something like this again. He was going to be there, and she wasn't going to be able to distance herself from him. He quickly finished washing her and rinsing the soap from her skin.

"Thank you." She turned her brown eyes to him, a small smile on her lips.

The sadness in her eyes touched something deep inside him. He was falling in love with her. He knew without a doubt he was crazy about her

"You don't have to thank me." His voice was gruff. He shut off the water and reached for a towel. He wrapped her up in it before reaching for one for himself.

They exited the shower and dried themselves off. He took her shower cap off and set it down on the counter. He took Nykee and led her by the hand to the bedroom.

Without a word, he assisted her into the bed and

climbed in with her. She took her rightful spot at his side. Karl wrapped his arms around her and pulled her into him, and tucked the blanket around them. A shudder went through her as she settled into his embrace. Minutes later, her breaths evened out, and she drifted off to sleep with Karl not too far behind her.

18

Nykee stared down at the man sleeping beside her. She'd woken up, surprisingly refreshed. After her night at the police station, coming home to find Karl waiting for her was a surprise. But she shouldn't be. He was determined and straightforward. He'd made no qualms about his desire to have her.

She reached out and trailed a finger along his jawline. The hairs on from his dark shadow were prickly. A shiver went through her at the thought of feeling the scratchy hairs against the smooth skin on her thighs.

But she pushed those thoughts down.

They needed to have the talk.

Karl's eyelashes fluttered opened, and his hazel eyes settled on her.

"Morning," his deep voice rumbled.

He snuck an arm around her and pulled her flush to him. Her naked breasts rested on his muscular form. Nykee loved the feeling of her bare skin against his. Her nipples were erect and pressed against his warmth. They were sensitive, and she just wanted to rub herself against him to enjoy the enhanced pleasure of them.

A sexy grin spread across his face. "Whatcha staring at me for?"

She tried to keep from smiling, but she just couldn't. That hand of his slid down her back and rested along the swell of her ass. It settled on her and gave a possessive squeeze as if to wordlessly claim her as his. Her core clenched, loving the feel of his hands on her.

"I'm trying to see if I should have you checked out by a psychologist," she murmured.

"For what?" His eyes widened.

He settled back against the pillows, taking her with him. How could this man just wake up and look so damn sexy? She squeezed her thighs together in an attempt to control the hussy inside her and tried to think of the conversation she needed to have with him, but he was making it hard.

"Because I wasn't a good person. I have this

history that will continue to follow me, and you'd be crazy to be with me," she whispered. Her smile slowly faded as she held his gaze.

He reached up and cupped her face. She leaned into it, loving the feeling of his warm palm on her face. He was too good to be true.

"None of us are the same person we were in the past," he whispered. His smile disappeared, and his eyes became so serious. "We wouldn't be human if we didn't grow and change. Do you know who you are?"

She nodded, too choked up to speak. His gaze didn't waver while he studied her. It was crazy how this man was making her see a future she never thought she'd have.

"And is the woman I've come to care for the real you?"

His thumb stroked her skin, sending a tremor through her. Again, she jerked her head up and down. He was tearing down each wall she had built. Nykee's vision blurred from unshed tears that developed.

He guided her down to him and pressed a soft kiss to her lips. "Then that is who I want. Do you want me?"

"Yes," she sighed. There was no denying it. This time Nykee kissed him. Their discussion wasn't going how she imagined it would have. This kiss was full of all the emotions swirling around in her. She needed him. He balanced out all the doubt and hesitation she held inside her. She pulled back and rested her forehead on his. "I'm just scared."

"Of what?" His hand trailed up her back slowly.

He adjusted them to where she lay in the crook of his arm. She felt safe and secure in his embrace. It hadn't been often she'd had this feeling from a male who wasn't related to her. Her ex never comforted her, never cared what she thought, and certainly didn't make her feel good about herself. He just took and took from her until she had no more to give.

But Karl, he gave her his all.

"Losing what we had," she admitted. Already, in their short time, she wanted a future with Karl. She craved his touch, his voice, his kisses, and his body inside hers.

Was this love?

She had thought she was in love before with Foster, but she'd learned that wasn't love.

One doesn't abuse the one they claim you love. One doesn't allow people to use the one they love, and they certainly don't risk the life of the one they love.

She had been in an abusive relationship and had never realized it until it was too late. She had been groomed to think that what they had was normal.

Everything with Karl was different. He was

genuine and true. He cared for her and would never hurt her. She was his primary concern. Nykee had never had a man put her first, and it was the best feeling she'd ever had.

How could she throw that away? She would be a fool to not fight for what she had with Karl.

"I'm not going anywhere." He tipped her chin up, making her meet his gaze. "Do you think I would truly walk away from you? You have filled my mind from the moment we met. I'm crazy over you, and there's no way I would just leave and forget you."

"I'm crazy about you, too." She covered his hand with hers. It was the truth. She'd thought of nothing but him since they'd met. She smiled softly and blinked back the tears. She was not going to cry.

"Good. Now that we got all of that behind us, there is something that I must do."

He rolled them over until she was on her back and he was braced over her. She giggled, loving his playful side. He bent down and nuzzled his face between her breasts. He inhaled sharply and groaned.

"I will never get enough of your scent."

"What are you talking about?" She laughed, watching him breathe her in. He was clearly going crazy. They'd showered last night, and what he was smelling was her shower gel, but she wasn't going to break the mood and try to tell him that.

Let him think her natural essence was sweet almonds and vanilla.

He slid down her body and pushed her legs apart. Karl settled in the valley of her thighs with his face level with her center. Her smile faded once she understood his intention. Her breath caught in her throat at the sight of him staring at her core. Her body flushed, a warm sensation starting at the top of her head down to the tips of her toes.

Karl used his finger to part her folds while his focus was locked on her. She couldn't look away from him if she tried.

He teased her clit, rubbing it softly. A moan slipped from her. She widened her legs to allow him to have full access to her. It was a sensual sight to watch him take his time learning her. She bit her lip at the feeling of his finger circling her entrance that was growing wet. It pushed forward inside her.

"I love everything about you. Your smile, the scent of your skin, and the taste of you." He pulled his finger free and sucked the slickness from his skin.

Her mouth dropped open slightly. His head dropped down, his lips capturing her little bundle of nerves.

Nykee's body arched off the mattress, a cry tearing from her lips. He took his time pleasuring her. She writhed on the bed as his fingers and mouth went to work. He brought her to the brink of her orgasm, only to pull back. She grew frantic needing that euphoric feeling of bliss. An electric current burned along her skin. Karl's tongue was magical, and the sensations it delivered were to die for. If the pleasure he brought her was a slice of heaven, she'd do whatever she could to hold on to it.

She opened her eyes and glanced down at him, finding him watching her. Lust burned heavy in his gaze. Her heart raced at the expression of pure hunger in his expression. His breaths came out in pants. The veins along his neck were prominent. His eyes darkened as he glanced back down at her soaked center.

"Why did you stop?" she gasped. Her body was drawn tight, and it wouldn't take much for her to fall over the cliff into ecstasy. Her core pulsated with the need for release.

"I want to feel you come on my dick," he murmured.

He sat back on his haunches, his gaze dropping back to her. She was sure she made one hell of a sight. Her legs were spread wide, and trails of her juices slid along the crease of her ass. Her hair was probably standing up every kind of way, but with the way Karl was looking at her, he liked what he saw.

Her gaze was drawn to his hand encircling his

hard and swollen member. His hand slid along the length of it, while he didn't take his eyes off her. She was mesmerized by him pleasuring himself. She wanted to see him finish, but now wasn't the time. There was a heavy ache inside her to have Karl's cock sinking into her.

He didn't make her wait long.

He nudged the head of his length to her entrance before pressing forward. Nykee held her breath at the feeling of his thick cock stretching her out. It was the best feeling she had ever experienced. There was a slight pain, but she welcomed it. He paused once he was fully seated in her.

Their eyes connected, and something magical passed through them. Nykee couldn't describe it, but she felt a connection to Karl. It was like a light had gone off in her brain.

He was the one for her.

That was it. She knew there would be no other. He had her heart, and she would gladly give it to him. She was in love with this man who wanted to be with her with all of her faults and history.

He didn't care.

He just wanted her.

Nykee slid her hands along the smooth lines of his back, memorizing the feel of the taut muscles. His hips moved, setting a hard and fast rhythm.

Nykee met him with each thrust. They rocked against each other, seeking that final destination they would reach together.

The sound of their lovemaking filled the air. Sighs, pants, and groans joined the rhythmic slapping of skin. Karl captured her lips in an earth-shattering kiss. He possessed her, and there was no resistance on her part. She freely gave herself to him.

It didn't take Nykee long to crest with Karl right behind her, shouting his release.

⚜

"I NEED MY CAR, KARL." NYKEE FOLDED HER ARMS in front of her.

She was thankful the moment Karl slid his shirt over his head. He'd been walking around her house shirtless, and it had left her tongue-tied. She couldn't stop staring at his perfect chest. He grinned at her and sauntered over to her.

"I can just take you to work tomorrow." He gathered her to him, his hands resting on her waist. He bent down and pressed a quick kiss on her lips.

She broke free of his grip and moved away. If she stay too much longer in his arms, they would end up back in her bed.

They had spent most of the day with their naked

bodies entwined together. She left the room with a smile on her face and headed down to the living room. Her bedroom was a trap. Karl was going to try to sweet talk her back out of her clothes.

"No, sir. You have to be at work too early in the morning. I don't do the ass crack of dawn," she hollered over her shoulder.

His deep chuckle followed behind her. It was growing late, and the sun was on its way down. She couldn't remember the last time she'd spent an entire day in the bed.

Not that Karl had let her get much sleep.

"And you promised me food," she grumbled. Her stomach chose that moment to growl. she went on the search for her favorite sandals that were supposed to be in the living room. She found them hiding halfway underneath her couch. She bent down and snatched them up.

"That I did. We can go now for dinner, then head to my place." Karl grabbed her from behind, wrapping his arms around her. He nuzzled his face in the crook of her neck.

"Where I will get my car and then I'll go home and you will stay at your home," she said. Her core clenched when he nipped her skin. The man had a way of eliciting things from her body that she didn't control.

"That's not what I want," he murmured, his lips brushing her skin.

She melted against him. The hard plains of his body complimented her curves. Where he was full-on muscle, she was soft and fluffy.

Sirens sounded outside her home. Nykee stiffened. Karl cursed and released her. He stalked over to window and pushed the curtains aside. Nykee's heart raced.

Not again.

Karl turned to her and shook his head.

"They're across the street," he said.

Nykee moved to stand next to him to have a look for herself. The police were in the driveway speaking with her neighbor. Her heart slowed. She turned to Karl with relief.

"You still want to get some food?" Karl slid his arm around her and pulled her in for a hug.

She was going to have to relax. Not all police sirens were for her.

"Yeah. Let's go, I'm starving." She sighed.

They quickly threw their shoes on and locked up the house. Karl escorted her to his truck and opened the door. Nykee couldn't help her curiosity. She paused next to the vehicle and looked across the street the deputies were speaking with the Chamberses.

She wondered what had happened and why the police had been called.

"Babe, let's go," Karl murmured.

He rested a hand on the small of her back and urged her to get inside. He helped her inside and shut the door. He jogged to the other side and got in. He started the engine and backed out. Nykee's nose was plastered to the window, her trying to take in the scene. They sped off down the street, and the last thing Nykee saw was the police entering Mrs. Chambers's home.

"Anywhere special you have in mind?" she asked. Nykee turned to face him. She was trying to the push scene from Mrs. Chambers's home away. She was sure everything would he okay.

"We could either hit up the Tipsy Cow or stop at the Farmhouse Diner." Karl glanced over at her.

She grimaced, not really wanting to go to either. She was almost tempted to suggest going a town over but that would take too long. This was the downside of living in a small town.

"Or we can pick something up to go from the diner."

He must have seen her face. Picking up the food sounded much better than sitting down to eat.

"Let's do that," Nykee murmured.

Eating at his place wouldn't be so bad. She turned

around and stared out the window and had to figure how she was going to be able to leave Karl's home. The smile that crept on his face was suspicious. He had something planned up his sleeve. She tried to hide her smile because she was sure whatever he had planned, she was going to fully enjoy it.

19

Karl held the door open to the Farmhouse Diner for Nykee. She breezed past him and entered. He sensed she was still bothered by the sight of the police at her neighbor's home. When the sirens had sounded, her body had grown tense, and he'd immediately known she was thinking they were coming for her. The fear in her eyes had him feeling protective of her, and he vowed to always be at her side.

"Hey, Karl, y'all eating here tonight?" Diane, the host, asked. She greeted him with a smile but caste a wary eye toward Nykee.

He moved to stand next to her and took her hand, entwining their fingers together. Diane's eyebrows shot up high at the move. He pulled Nykee close and pressed a kiss to her forehead. He wanted everyone to know that she was his woman.

"We're going to order our meal to go." His voice came out gruff. He didn't appreciate how she hadn't even spoken to Nykee.

"Y'all can head over to the bar and order over there." Diana said.

She smiled at them, but Karl didn't return the gesture. She had blatantly disrespected Nykee, and he was biting his tongue to keep from saying anything. He just wanted to get their food and go.

"Come on," he murmured.

He towed Nykee behind him. The diner was busy for a Sunday evening. It was probably best they took their food to go. There looked to a be wait, and he didn't want to stay any longer than they needed to. Once he got Nykee to his house, he would be trying to convince her to spend the night. Her bag from the other night was still there. She could wash whatever she needed so they could go to work in the morning. He didn't want them to sleep separate. He was getting used to having her at his side at night and didn't think he would be able to sleep soundly without her.

Was it too soon to bring up moving in together?

Nykee would probably think so, but he didn't.

There was no doubt he wanted to take their relationship a step further.

He would just have to convince Nykee.

There were a few patrons at the bar enjoying their meal. Karl leaned against the counter and reached for a menu. Nykee took a seat in the chair next to him. Her mouth was pressed together in a firm line. Something was bothering her. He leaned over and brought his arms around her with the menu so they could review it together.

She turned around and glanced at him with sadness in her eyes. The protective beast inside him stood to attention. He was immediately ready to defend her against whatever was bothering her.

"What is it?" he asked. He tightened his grip on her.

She pressed closer to him and exhaled.

"It's nothing," she replied.

But it didn't look to be nothing. Karl was no fool. She offered a smile, but it didn't connect with her eyes.

He looked around and caught quite a few people staring at them. The minute his gaze met the stares, they broke eye contact and turned away. He simmered, pissed that they would try to make her feel unwelcome.

"Are you worried about what people are thinking?" He rested his chin on her shoulder where his voice was kept low.

"Yeah. They always treat me different." She sniffed.

Unable to resist, he pressed a kiss to her cheek. Her big soulful eyes turned to him. His heart cracked at the pain in her brown orbs.

"I thought it was getting better the longer I was back. But with everything that is going on with the robberies the deputies keep trying to accuse me of, I guess I will get used to it. The town will always see me as a criminal."

This wasn't right. Shady Springs was her home, and she should feel comfortable in this town. Her family was here, her place of business...he was here.

Karl was going to make this right. He didn't know what he was going to do, but he'd damn sure make Nykee feel welcome and loved in her own town.

"You want to get out of here?" he asked. He wouldn't have a problem spending his money elsewhere. Nykee was his top priority, and he wanted her to feel safe and secure.

"No, let's just order something and go." She leaned back against him and flipped the menu open.

The waitress behind the counter finally came over to them and took their order.

"Hey, Julie. Put the television on the news," one

of the customers asked who was sitting at the counter.

"Sure, Henry." The waitress snagged the remote and changed the channel before disappearing through a set of doors that led to the kitchen.

The local news was just coming on. Karl and Nykee both froze and turned their attention to the television.

"Good evening, Shady Springs. My name is Jeff Grant," a handsome male newscaster announced.

"And I'm Christina Gomez," the female news correspondent said. The camera zeroed in on her. "We have breaking news. Tonight, deputies are requesting the help of Shady Springs citizens. There has been a series of break-ins and robberies going around our little town, and we need your help."

Nykee stiffened. Karl took her hand and dropped a kiss on the back of it. Neither of them had watched the news or knew much about what was going on.

"According to the sheriff's department, each of the robberies have been almost identical. The thieves target homes where families are away. When the residents return, they returned to their homes vandalized and privacy destroyed." Jeff gave a serious look into the camera.

Nykee glanced at Karl. He already knew what she was thinking.

This was what they were trying to blame on her.

"Is this why he was asking if my 'friends' were back in town?" she asked softly. She turned to him, anger lighting up her brown eyes. "From what they are describing, one person couldn't have done that."

The camera transitioned to a home that had Karl pausing. He jerked his chin toward the screen. Nykee turned around, a gasp escaping her. The house on the television was the one directly across the street from her home. There were several police cars parked in the yard and on the street in front of it. They hadn't been gone that long, and it looked like a circus.

A young female news reporter stood with a microphone interviewing a heavyset woman with short dark hair. Tears were running down the woman's face. She must be the homeowner.

"Mrs. Chambers. When you returned home, what did you find?" The young woman placed the mic in front of Nykee's neighbor.

Karl stared at the news reporter and couldn't put his finger on where he knew her from. Then it hit him. His brother had dated her for a moment. He'd brought her around a few times. She was a pretty cool girl, but things hadn't worked out between her and Kaden. If Karl remembered correctly, she and his brother were still friends.

"My house was trashed, and all of the doors were

closed. I haven't had a chance to see what all we're missing. Big things we noticed was a television that was in the kitchen." The woman appeared distraught. She blotted her eyes with tissue she held. "The only thing that was wasn't touched was the package left on my back porch. I had forgotten I'd ordered something, and the thieves didn't take it."

"Oh my god," Nykee breathed. She spun around to him with wide eyes.

"What is it?" he asked.

"The other day before I came over your house, there was a package on my porch that wasn't for me. It was Mrs. Chambers's. I walked it over to her house and dropped it off on the porch."

"What's wrong with that?"

"They are going to try to pin this on me. The lady who lives next door saw me walk in the back yard." Nykee hopped down from the chair. She gathered her purse and hefted it up on her shoulder, a determined expression on her face. "We have to go back there. I need to speak with Mrs. Chambers."

***

NYKEE FIDGETED WITH HER HANDS AS KARL DROVE her back to her home. She prayed Mrs. Chambers was still home. She had to let her know she was the one who'd put the package in her back yard. She thought of the day she'd been there and remembered how the dogs had been acting. They had been barking like crazy. Dusky, who she knew was barking. She hadn't thought twice about it, but normally he didn't bark at her. He'd been in her yard and knew her.

She wondered if the robbers had been in the house when she was dropping off the box. That was what Dusky was probably trying to tell her.

"Are you sure you want to speak with Mrs. Chambers?" Karl asked.

"Yeah. We know each other. I feel bad. She recently lost her daughter to cancer." Nykee sniffed. It had been sad. Her daughter had been in her mid-twenties and so full of life before she got sick. Dusky had been her daughter's dog, and he wasn't used to being caged up. He would always get loose and ended up across the street in her yard.

"Shit," Karl breathed.

"I just want to make sure she's okay and see if she needs anything," Nykee said. Mrs. Chambers was a sweet woman, and this was a horrible thing to have happened.

They drove in a silence and within minutes were pulling back into Nykee's driveway. The police and the media were still there. Not much happened in

Shady Springs, so it wasn't surprising that the news was trying to make the most of this story.

Nykee hopped out of the truck before Karl killed the engine. She left her purse in the vehicle and immediately headed toward the Chambers's home. She jogged across the street, ignoring the woman from the news station speaking with her cameraman by their white van.

"I'll be over there. I know her," Karl said, jerking his head toward the news van. He had his phone out and was texting someone.

"Okay." Nykee headed toward the front door and walked up the stairs. The police cruisers were empty. She arrived at the door and rang the doorbell. She stepped back and waited. Voices could be heard from inside, and soon, footsteps marched toward her.

The door swung open, and Mrs. Chambers stood before her with a surprised look on her face.

"Nykee, dear. How are you?" Mrs. Chambers asked. Her red eyes appeared kind, but there was a strain around them. She had been one of the few neighbors who'd spoken with Nykee since she'd moved in.

"I saw the police over here and just saw the news. I'm so sorry," Nykee rushed out.

Mrs. Chambers stepped out onto the porch with her and pulled the screen door shut. Nykee glanced inside and saw a few of the police walking through the house. From the little she could see of the home, things were thrown everywhere.

"Nothing for you to be sorry about." Mrs. Chambers waved her hands. She offered a small smile and reached up and tucked her hair behind her ears. "So far, nothing of importance was taken. We can replace the electronics they stole—"

"I wouldn't be sharing anything with her," Deputy Griffen said from the door. He glared at Nykee and leaned against the doorjamb.

"Excuse me? This is my neighbor. I can share what I want with her," Mrs. Chambers snapped. She spun around and motioned for him to leave them. "Shouldn't you be looking around and collecting evidence?"

Nykee smirked. It would appear as if Mrs. Chambers was a little pissed off at the deputy.

"Ma'am. With all due respect—"

"I don't want to hear it," Mrs. Chambers cut him off.

Nykee didn't feel sorry for the deputy at all. Someone had to put him in his place. If she tried it, she'd have handcuffs on her wrist in moments. Nykee stood there enjoying Mrs. Chambers laying into him.

"The news has been reporting these home invasions and robberies for weeks, and you still haven't caught the thieves. What's taking so long? It's not like much happens here in Shady Springs. This should be your primary focus. Now my home has been hit." Mrs. Chambers stood with her hands on her waist.

His jaw tightened. His gaze flicked to Nykee for a brief moment before returning to Mrs. Chambers.

"We are almost done here. We need to confirm when the package was delivered to your home," Griffen said.

"I'd have to check my delivery confirmation in my email," Mrs. Chambers said.

"I can tell you that," Nykee said.

Griffen and Mrs. Chambers turned to her.

"It was delivered to my house. When I got home from work, I found the box on my doorstep. I ran it over and placed it on the back porch," she admitted. She stood with her fingers entwined together in front of her. Nykee was nervous sharing this information, but it was the truth.

"Around what time was that?"

Nykee paused and thought about the time she'd arrived home. She shared with them what time she'd dropped the box off. Griffen pulled out his notepad and wrote down a few items.

"Thanks so much for dropping it off, Nykee. I appreciate it." Mrs. Chambers rested a hand on

Nykee's shoulder. She turned back to Griffen. "Is there anything else you need?"

"We've collected some fingerprints. We'll need to collect yours and everyone who has the right to be in the house so we can eliminate them."

"That's fine. When do you want to do this?" Mrs. Chambers asked.

Nykee turned around and leaned against the pillar, ignoring the rest of their conversation. She caught sight of Karl talking with the pretty news reporter. She beat down the slight form of jealousy that reared its ugly head. There was nothing to worry about. Karl was into her and had never even looked at another woman in her presence. They glanced over at her. The woman smiled and waved. Nykee returned the gesture.

Nykee jumped at the sound of the door opening and heavy footsteps behind her. She glanced over her shoulder to see the deputies coming out of the house carrying their equipment and items they had bagged up. She wondered if they had fully investigated anything else that had happened or had they just zeroed in on her.

She truly doubted they had. If they had, they would have never approached her with their weak claims. Her father had spoken with Mr. Moss while they were processing her for release, and apparently they did not have anything suggestive that she was involved with the robberies. She was to call him on Monday so they could further discuss what had happened.

Karl and the news crew walked over to them. He motioned for her to join them at the bottom of the stairs.

"Nykee, this is Natalie. She used to date my brother, Kaden," he introduced them.

Nykee smiled and shook the woman's hand. Nykee didn't have a good history with the media. When she was on trial, they had painted her as a cold, callous woman, the girlfriend of the infamous gangster. Natalie's smile was warm and welcoming. Nykee didn't get the sense she was like all the reporters who had followed her before.

"It's so nice to meet you. This is my camera man, Joe." Natalie motioned to the man standing next to her with a small camera hanging down in his hand. Natalie turned to Nykee and lowered her voice. "Karl told me what the police have been putting you through."

"Is that so," she murmured. Nykee's gaze cut to Karl who came to stand beside her.

"And I want to help," Natalie said. Her lips pursed together in a firm line. "I've been reporting on these robberies, and this is the first that I've heard that they have been targeting you with no evidence."

"I guess since I have a history—"

"That is not how they should be conducting investigations by just assuming," Natalie cut her off. She smiled and reached out, taking Nykee's hand in hers, and gave it a quick squeeze. "Don't worry. We're going to force them to do their job. They've gotten lazy in the past few years, and we'll make them do their damn jobs."

"I'm innocent," Nykee whispered softly, not wanting Griffen or the other deputies to hear her.

"I know who you are. I followed your trial. I was in college and studied your case. I actually did a paper on you," Natalie admitted sheepishly and reached up to tuck her dark hair behind her ear. "This doesn't fit your profile from back then. They are just lazy. Don't you worry you about anything."

"Thank you." Nykee was floored. She didn't know what to think. This woman knew who she was and had studied her? That was a first for her.

Karl gave her another squeeze and dropped a kiss to the top of her head.

Natalie tossed her a wink and spun around, taking a few steps. She stopped and turned back.

"Any chance you have openings? I just adopted a miniature collie, and she needs haircut."

"I'm sure we do. Just call the shop, and we'll get you in. I don't have a card on me."

"Ha, you do realize I'm the news, right? I know everything about this town. I'll give you a call." Natalie smiled before continuing on over to the deputies.

Nykee didn't know what to think of this turn of events. How was Natalie going to help her?

"We need to talk," Nykee tipped her head back to look at Karl.

He tried to appear innocent. It was no wonder he hadn't really argued with her in coming back here.

"I'm not above fighting dirty to get them off your back." A seriousness came over him. He caressed her chin with his free hand. "You matter to me, and I want you at peace here."

It was official.

She was in love with him.

"Deputy Griffen, I have a few more questions for you and then I should be done here," Natalie announced, arriving at the deputy's cruiser.

Joe stood next to her, hefting his camera onto his shoulder and pointing it at Griffen.

Nykee glanced over at Karl who slid a hand along her shoulders and gave her a squeeze and a reassuring nod. What had he discussed with Natalie?

"Sure, Miss Gallagher. How can I help you?"

Griffen shut the trunk and turned to them. He had a false smile on his lips.

Nykee was nauseated by the look. He appeared as if he really wanted to help Natalie, but Nykee was sure it was because the cameras were rolling and he'd be in the public eye.

"Does the community of Shady Springs know that police have been targeting a poor innocent woman instead of doing their job and investigating these robberies?" Natalie placed the microphone near the deputy's mouth.

Nykee's mouth dropped open. She froze in place, unable to believe what she'd just heard.

"Say what? Who the hell told you that?" Griffen sputtered.

"And the woman you are targeting by making false claims is a woman who has paid her debt to society and now is a respectable member of our community," Natalie snapped.

Nykee's eyebrows jerked up. It was amazing to watch the deputy stammer and stumble over his words. His face was bright as he responded.

"We have committed to keeping this community safe. The woman in question—"

"Does not fit the motive of these crimes. I'm sure you are well aware of her background and can admit, this is different."

"Yes, but—"

"And you still harassed her." Natalie waved to the cameraman and dropped her microphone. "Is this the story you want me to run?"

"Of course not," Griffen snapped. He glared over at Nykee, a sneer on his lips.

Karl stiffened and stalked over to him. Nykee took off and grabbed his arm, trying to pull him back, but he was like a runaway bull. She stumbled behind him and stopped at his side, ready to jump in front of him if need be.

"Then do your damn job and leave Nykee alone," Karl growled. He stood toe to toe with the deputy, staring him directly in the eye.

Nykee's heart pounded. She didn't want him to get thrown in jail for assaulting an officer. The other deputies stood to attention, eyeing Karl. He stood a few inches taller than Griffen and was pure muscle, while the deputy was older and soft around the middle. He wouldn't stand a chance in an altercation with Karl.

"How about this. We do a story on the evidence you found and we'll air it as a story on the evening news to plead the cases. So far you haven't shared much with the public. They need to know," Natalie said.

Griffen broke the staring contest with Karl and

focused on Natalie. He paused, thinking on what she'd said, but the news reporter continued.

"Either I can show how hard the police is working to make the townspeople of Shady Springs safe or I can do an exclusive on how you are preying on a black woman and falsely accusing her of crimes you know she didn't commit and using her as a scapegoat."

The silence was deafening. Nykee didn't move a muscle. This was heavy. The news could definitely spin the story any way they saw fit, and for the townspeople, they would believe the media. What had been shared before? Nykee kicked herself that she didn't watch the news. She vowed from now on that she would so she would know what was going on in her town. She had kept herself so isolated, she was completely in the dark about the events that went around.

"Well. Miss Gallagher, you know we always want the stories about the sheriff's department to be good. Bad media could be damaging." He rested his hands on his tool belt and cleared his throat.

"Then you tell me when to come down to the station, and I promise, I will share a story so enlightening that the townspeople will get behind you and help find the culprits who are doing this."

Relief filled Nykee. Was this truly over? That

easy? She would never have went to the media for help. The thought of reaching out to them brought on hives. They hadn't been kind to her in the past.

"Let's go." Karl took her hand and threw Griffen another heated glare before leading her away.

She followed behind him, heart pounding so hard, she would have sworn it was going to push through her chest. She took a second to look over her shoulder and saw Natalie still speaking with Griffen.

Something came over Nykee. A calmness she couldn't explain washed over her. She held on to Karl's hand and allowed him to lead her back to the truck.

"Where are we going?" she asked.

They stopped next to the passenger door. His gaze was locked on her. The cold hardness she had witness roll over his gaze lifted. He reached down and cupped her cheek.

"I still need to feed you."

Her stomach chose that moment to agree by rumbling. He grinned and stepped closer to her, pushing her back against the truck. He leaned down and covered her mouth with his. The kiss was soft and slow. Nykee's knee grew weak. She leaned into him as he took his time exploring her mouth. He broke the kiss and rested his forehead against hers.

"What was that for?" she whispered. Her hands

settled on his waist as she tried to catch her breath. She'd felt the love that he had for her in the kiss. Nykee was in love with him, and she would wait till the perfect time to tell him. With everything he'd done for her so they could be together, she knew he loved her. He'd shown it with his actions. She'd be patient and wait for the day they would openly share their feelings.

Karl stared into her eyes, his sexy grin settling on his lips.

"Just because."

EPILOGUE

Karl settled back on the couch with his cold beer in his hand. Nykee came to settle next to him. She tucked her feet underneath her and leaned into him. It had been about a month since her neighbor's house had been robbed. He reached for the remote and turned the television on. He'd gotten a text from Natalie for them to tune in tonight. There had been a breakthrough in the case, apparently.

Ever since Karl and Nykee had run into Natalie at Nykee's neighbor's home, the police had been more vocal about the investigations on all of the homes that had been burglarized. Natalie had been covering the stories and sharing what the police was finding.

No longer were the police antagonizing Nykee.

He was glad that his brother and ex-girlfriend

were still on good terms. He had shot off a text to Kaden to be sure before he'd approached Natalie, and Kaden had confirmed they were. It made it a little easier to approach her. Had they been on the outs, it may not have gone so well.

But thankfully, Natalie had a heart of gold and was a pit pull when it came to the mistreatment of female ex-cons trying to make a better life for themselves. She had recently requested to speak with Nykee about her experience. She was going to do a special on life after prison for women, and Nykee had agreed to be interviewed.

"Hurry up and turn the channel," Nykee urged.

"Hold your horses, woman." He chuckled. He took a sip of his beer and finally found the correct channel. One thing they had both started doing was staying in tune with what was going on in their little town.

Nykee had sort of moved into his home, even though she wouldn't admit it. He wasn't going to complain. Half of his dresser and closet were filled with her clothes.

But she didn't live here. She just kept things over for when she spent the night, which was every night.

He bit back a grin and glanced over at her. She had her hair in two braids and appeared happy. There was definitely a difference between this Nykee and the one he'd first met.

The love he had for her choked him for a moment. He thought of the purchase he'd just made a week ago that would make their relationship official. He'd already spoken with her family who were excited that he was going to propose.

The words 'breaking news' flashed across the screen.

"Why am I so nervous?" Nykee whispered. Her eyes grew wide as she watched the news story start.

"Don't be." He dropped a kiss on the back of her hand and settled it on his leg.

"Good evening, Shady Springs. We have breaking news that we are sure you are ready to hear," the newscaster stated. She held a serious look while the camera focused on her. "Our lead correspondent, Natalie Gallagher, has the latest on the multiple robberies that have been occurring around town."

The screen cut to Natalie who was in a red dress with her long tresses settled around her shoulders. She sat behind a desk, an intense look on her face.

"The sheriff's department has finally cracked the case on the sporadic robberies that have occurred. The community of Shady Springs should feel safe and sleep much better at night," Natalie began. She turned, and the camera followed her as she continued. "Apparently, Shady Springs was being used as an initiation site for new members of The Black Aces. Multiple members of the gang have been arrested and charged with burglary. Over fifteen members are behind bars tonight thanks to the dedication of the sheriff's department who has worked tirelessly to make our town safe once again."

"So what you are telling us, is that the people of Shady Springs were being terrorized as an initiation ritual for some criminals?" the anchorwoman asked.

"That's correct, Susan." Natalie nodded. "They traveled down from Colorado Springs, have a target home or business, break in, take what they want, and then leave immediately."

Photos of the arrested gang members flashed onto the screen.

"It's truly over," Nykee breathed. Tears streamed down her face.

He turned to her and began wiping them away. He hated seeing her like this.

"It should have never started." He tipped her chin up and pressed a gentle kiss to her lips. Aside from the media threatening to expose the sheriff's department for their treatment of Nykee, her lawyer had sent a cease and desist letter to them, threatening to sue if they continued their treatment of her.

Deputy Griffen even offered an official apology to

her the day he'd announced his retirement. It had been aired on the news. He hadn't said her name, but Karl and Nykee knew who he had been speaking of.

Nykee inhaled and smiled.

"That's my girl," he murmured and dropped another kiss to her lips. He couldn't keep his hands off her, and ever since she'd begun spending the night every night, he didn't have to.

He thought of the small black box he'd hidden in the house and figured now would be the best time. This ruckus was finally behind them, and they could move forward with their lives. Nykee's business had blossomed, and she was in the process of hiring another groomer to help. Life was going great.

"I'll be right back. Gotta pee," he lied. He finished off the last of his beer and took the empty bottle with him.

Nykee settled back and reached for the remote and began flipping the channels. He tossed the bottle away in the garbage in the kitchen before heading back to his—their—bedroom.

Karl returned with the little box in his shirt pocket. Nykee was engrossed in some action-packed movie. He knelt down on the floor in front of her, blocking the television.

"Hey, move, big head. I can't see." Nykee laughed. She tried to push him out of the way, but something on his face must had given her pause. "What are you doing?"

"Something I've been dying to do," he rasped. He cleared his throat that suddenly became dry. He had practiced repeatedly since he'd made the purchase, and now that he had finally decided to do it, he was tongue-tied.

"And what is that?" Her eyes grew wide as saucers when he pulled the little black box out of his pocket. "Karl," she sighed.

He took her hand in his and brought it up to his lips. He met her eyes, a smile forming on his lips. He wasn't going to worry about the right words. He was going to just go with what was deep in his heart.

"Nykee Nash. From the moment we first met, you left one hell of an impression on me. I knew instantly I needed to get to know you," he began.

"Oh my God," she exclaimed. She sat up even further on the couch, her gaze locked on him. She didn't breathe while waiting for him to continue.

"And once I did, I fell in love with you." Karl opened the black velvet box holding the three-carat diamond ring he'd purchased for her.

His mother had helped him pick it out. There was no way that Billie was going to let him make this big of a purchase without being involved once he had told her he was going to propose to Nykee.

"Karl, it's beautiful." Tears streamed down Nykee's face again.

He took the ring out and picked up Nykee's hand.

"Nykee Nash. I want to spend the rest of my life with you. There's nothing that will keep me from you, nothing that would allow me to give up on what we have. You are everything that I want and need. Will you marry me?" he asked.

"Yes!"

Nykee launched herself at him, wrapping her arms around his neck. She was half laughing, half crying. He brought her flush to him and breathed in her scent. She pulled back and held out her hand, watching as he slid the ring onto her finger. It was the perfect fit.

Nykee cupped his face in her hands and rested her forehead to his.

"You are everything that I want, too." She sniffed. She opened her beautiful brown eyes, and he again fell in love with her in that moment. "I love you, too, you stubborn man."

He covered her mouth with his. He stood and lifted her into his arms and carried her through the house to their bedroom. He was going to take his time showing her how much he loved her.

A NOTE FROM THE AUTHOR

Dear reader,

I hope you enjoyed Karl and Nykee's story as much as I did. I have enjoyed writing the Blazing Eagle Ranch series so much. These two hold a special spot in my heart. I hope you loved them as much as I do.

As always, if you want more from my series, leave a review letting me know that!

Love,

Peyton

She was his best friend's sister and should have been off-limits.

Rashad Mays was a ranch hand on the Blazing Eagle Ranch. He had grown up in Shady Springs and had no intention of leaving. This was his home, and he was ready to settle down. Only the woman that captured his eye was the sister of his best friend, Nate.

There were unspoken rules between friends when it came to their little sisters--don't touch.

Yani Polk was not like other women. She didn't chase after cowboys for a casual roll in the hay. She was a lady. Sexy, curvy, successful, and currently the star of his late-night fantasies.

He'd thought he would be able to push her out of his mind, but when she came strolling onto the ranch, he couldn't resist. Her smile and the gentle sway of her hips called to him.

The sizzling attraction was too great to resist. Rashad did the unthinkable. He broke the rules.

Yani was the woman for him, and he was willing to fight to prove it.

⚜

Want to read Knockin' the Boots? Download it today!

ABOUT THE AUTHOR

USA TODAY bestselling author, Peyton Banks, is the alter ego of a city girl who is a romantic at heart. Her mornings consist of coffee and daydreaming up the next steamy romance book ideas. She loves spinning romantic tales of hot alpha males and the women they love. Make sure you check her out!

Sign up for Peyton's Newsletter to find out the latest releases, giveaways and news! Visit www.peyton banks.com/newsletter to sign up!

Want to know the latest about Peyton Banks? Follow her online:

Roping a Cowboy

Country at Heart

Cowboy, Take Me Away

Hard to Forget

<u>Special Weapons & Tactics Series</u>

Dirty Tactics (Special Weapons & Tactics 1)

Dirty Ballistics (Special Weapons & Tactics 2)

Dirty Operations (Special Weapons & Tactics 3)

Dirty Alliance (Special Weapons & Tactics 4)

Dirty Justice (Special Weapons & Tactics 5)

Dirty Trust (Special Weapons & Tactics 6)

Dirty Secrets (Special Weapons & Tactics 7)

Dirty Ultimatum (Special Weapons & Tactics 8)

<u>SWAT boxset, books 1-3</u>

<u>Trust & Honor Series (BWWM)</u>

Dallas

Dalton

<u>A Langdale Christmas</u>

The Christmas Secret

The Christmas Wish

The Christmas Gift

<u>Interracial Romances (BWWM)</u>

Pieces of Me

Hard Love

Retain Me

Silent Deception

<u>African American Romance</u>

Breaking The Rules

<u>Mafia Romance</u>

Unexpected Allies (The Tokhan Bratva 1)

www.ingramcontent.com/pod-product-compliance
Lightning Source LLC
Chambersburg PA
CBHW061645190726
48289CB00006B/1752